The Price
of the
Muse

Lee Hansen

*This book is self-published and is available through the author. If you
have an interest in this work, or other works by me, please email*

lee@thepriceofthemuse.com

ISBN: 0988345714
ISBN-13: 978-0-9883457-1-3

DEDICATION

My first novel is dedicated to my family –
Kailey, Nicolas, and Hillari. You encouraged me and
believed in me every step of the way.

My wish is that the hours I spent away from us to
write this book will now come back as
days and months of joy and happiness.

Part I – The Discovery

Chapter 1

Luka Meiter sipped his coffee on the broken patio of the old bakery. It was a bright, beautiful, cool June morning, a welcome and unexpected respite from the gray drizzle that had accompanied his drive home yesterday. He closed his eyes and raised his head to let the sun warm his face, and imagined the sound of tourists' footsteps clacking across the cobblestones of the old town square, as they stopped for picnic supplies, on the way to the Alps, on to Austria and France. Unfortunately those happy sounds of activity would never arrive for yet another summer.

Even the muffled gunfire that had rattled on to the south for the past two weeks was gratefully absent this morning. The last desperate push of the German troops back down valley and into the Arden in April had been a failure—although no one else around him knew that, at least not yet. The sound of shelling could be heard in the evenings, getting closer, and much sooner than expected. Shortly the German guerilla commandos would appear in the village upon their retreat to Berlin. They would come in the name of the Fatherland

and patriotism, but they would also ransack the already meager shops for food and provisions, rumor and stories, sifting for any clue of traitors and spies. They would leave nothing behind for the advancing Allies to find but stunned and angry villagers, sabotage, mines, and the occasional sniper.

Luka could hear Claudia humming from the back of her little café. It rose over the clattering of her mixing and kneading as she coaxed the bulgur flour and dried raisins into sweet muffins. Sneaking the rationed food stocks home with him had been a risk, but the flour was good and dry, no mold (such a rarity these days); and the raisins plumped up nicely when soaked in water. Besides, it was good strategy to have Claudia in debt to him, a respected shop owner and long-standing member of the little hamlet.

It was 1944, and Luka was relieved to see the end of the war finally at hand. The rationing, the propaganda, the constant smoke black from the kerosene lanterns he used to read by at night; being suddenly stuck in god-knows-where from lack of petrol, all that coming to an end. The frustrations of living and working in this torn and ravaged land would soon be a terrible memory. He imagined being able to move about Germany again without having to stop at checkpoints, no more bribes, no more papers checked—and stamped—and checked again.

Luka sighed. This hint of coming freedom from the war wouldn't come quickly, and it had already exacted such a high price. So many friends lost, and not just casualties of the fighting. The oppression, the ever-present fear of being caught saying the wrong thing to the wrong person, the hammering nightly artillery as the Allied advance approached, the surprise troop sweeps—all served to very effectively unnerve the populace and bolster the illusion of strength and stability. So many of his friends and acquaintances of the past few years were now gone, either through death or by simply leaving the country ahead of the waves of destruction that were finally coming home to roost.

More and more the whispers of the coming Nazi fall grew. You couldn't pick it out from the ragged newsletters that were still in print, and you couldn't glean it from the official radio broadcasts that gloated over the storied victories. But Luka knew from his own contacts and couriers just how close the Allied troops were; and not only were they close, their numbers were massive. He kept his knowledge quietly his own, but the truth was growing obvious from the battle that could be heard approaching from the south. Even his friend Nick the tobacconist had finally summoned up the courage to ask what Luka knew. Luka, the traveler, the smuggler, the man with money, surely he knew.

Like always, Luka lied, just enough. Enough to appear a part of the scared populace.

He shook his head, stretched and yawned out loud, an attempt to clear his mind of these rattled thoughts. He could hear the cackle of magpies in the clock tower across the square. Just then Claudia appeared through the doorway with a sweet muffin and another tiny cup of boiled espresso. "Here we are," she sang as she placed the plate on the table in front of him.

She patted him on the shoulder and continued, "I can't thank you enough for the flour. I'll be able to sell scones in the square this afternoon."

"You'll have the whole town here this morning once the smell reaches their windows," he assured her.

She laughed and patted him again, turning to head through the doorway and back to her baking.

Just as he heard Claudia's foot click onto the shop tile, Luka saw a man in a yellow-and-red checkered coat appear on the opposite side of the square, walking out from the shadow of the church into the bright daylight.

"Oh...my...this is it," the man stammered, looking around wildly.

Even though he was at least thirty meters away, Luka could clearly hear the man's voice carried by the crisp morning air over the empty cobblestones. He locked in on the man at once.

"Oh yes...yes!" he was now bent over, half laughing, and half crying, as if washed over by a great relief.

"Oh yes...unbelievable," he continued. The man was leaning into the side of the church for support, catching his breath, gazing around and above, like a child in awe at his surroundings.

"OH...and there YOU are...HA HA," he shouted in delight, spying Luka from across the square. He let go of the side of the church and began hobbling directly toward Luka and the café, smiling an enormous toothy grin.

Luka shot to his feet at the sudden realization that he was the target of the odd man's approach. He reached instinctively to his black overcoat draped across the chair to his right and felt for the Luger in the upper inside pocket, but just as instantly realized that he had left the loaded pistol in his room, believing it unneeded on such a serene morning.

"Damn," Luka muttered, that was a mistake. He turned back to scan the man still hobbling toward him.

"Oh yes...HA...so unbelievable, but then...I saw this...yes? How could it be any other way...HA HA."

The man coming at him was young, mid-twenties. We wore a woolen hunting jacket; an old one, checkered yellow and red that appeared too big for him. The sleeves hung off of his arms, partially hiding his hands. He had on dark blue trousers and worn black boots, the left pants leg shredded and torn below the knee. Yellow matted hair, and a full growth of unkempt beard covered his face. Tied to his waist was a dirty-white bag with something inside, swinging wildly as he moved; and he struggled as he walked, with a clear limp to his left leg. The limp had certainly been with him for some time, for he neither grimaced nor slowed as he closed the distance to the café. But his eyes were what unnerved Luka most; there was clear determination, and a wildness, a craziness to his look. The combination of odd, tattered clothes, staggering gait, and wild gaze made the man appear like a mad clown, sprung from some circus nightmare, striding into center ring.

Luka quickly glanced around to see if others were witnessing this absurd display. There was no one else in the square to either side or behind the man in the checkered coat. The earliness of the day could work to his advantage, but then he heard the gasp and a crash behind him, and turned to see Claudia standing in the shop doorway with her hand covering her mouth in astonishment. She was staring directly at the mad man and had dropped a plate of scones. Claudia quickly looked to Luka for reassurance, and with terror in her voice cried, "Luka...who is that? What is he doing?"

Luka spun back. The man had closed half the distance across the square already. There were few options that wouldn't arouse suspicion with Claudia as a witness, and even fewer without his Luger, and nothing else was coming to him in the moment...except to run.

Luka hurdled the short railing lining the patio and bolted for the street entrance just two shops down. As he ran he could hear the approaching man's tone change from jittery laughter to fear.

"Oh...OH NO! No, please...Herr Meiter PLEASE...please don't run," he shouted. But Luka didn't hesitate and didn't look back. He covered the short sprint to the street in a matter of seconds and ducked around the corner. His confronter was still coming. The checkered man's gait had now changed; Luka could hear the walk-thump, walk-thump of a half-run. And he was still shouting.

"I'VE COME ALL THIS WAY...TO FIND YOU" the man was yelling, and now he was beginning to gasp. "I mean you no harm...you see...I've seen all this...it's really quite amazing...LET ME EXPLAIN."

His footsteps grew closer. Luka sprinted again, down the side street. Halfway down the strasse he stopped and watched the strange man clear the corner.

"Oh...Oh please stop!"

"WHO ARE YOU?" Luka shouted.

"Erik...my name is Erik...Oh yes...please stop...I don't run so well...as I used to."

"DON'T COME ANY CLOSER," Luka commanded. "WHAT DO YOU WANT FROM ME?"

The hobbling man replied, "I know who you are...You are Luka Meiter, yes?...from here, Trier...but you're really not... not German...oh no, ha."

The hairs on the back of Luka's neck stood on end. How could this man whom he had never seen before possibly know that?

Glancing up he noted several apartment windows lining the street, some already opened to the warm morning, but saw no one. The yelling was sure to bring someone out soon. He quickly spied the entrance to an alleyway just ahead and across the street. That alley was narrow and long, lined on either side with shops and apartments above, but if he was quick he could get down the length of the alley before it emptied onto the next street, and get the checkered man out of the open street. Luka ran for the alley but turned to make sure the man would see him enter. He stopped, pressed to the wall at the corner, and listened for his pursuer.

"OH NO... I'm sorry...but I don't care...NO...I DON'T CARE WHO YOU REALLY ARE," the man shouted.

He was following. Luka began making his way down the alley, moving slowly enough to keep the hobbling man in view; the next street crossing was about ninety meters ahead.

The man in the checkered coat rounded the corner after Luka, and staggered. For a moment he appeared as if he would fall, but slowly he gathered himself and followed down the alley. He was clearly winded and dazed, and still staggering. "I'm sorry...you see...I need your help...as an art dealer...you can get...my painting for me...it's most incredible...unbelievable...please let me explain."

Luka was now five meters from the end of the alley. "STOP! DON'T COME ANY CLOSER," he turned and shouted back. At the far end of the alley Luka saw a young boy appear on a balcony, searching up and down the alley for the source of the early morning commotion.

"Damn," whispered Luka. His options were rapidly narrowing.

Then suddenly the crazy man stopped. "I'm sorry...I've scared you...Yes...oh certainly, yes. But it's the most...fantastic thing...you really aren't going to believe...I didn't believe it at first...like a dream," and the man broke into broken laughter.

"You see...it's my painting...I stumbled across it...and you're in it, you see...well, it's...I didn't paint it...but it's me...and you...exactly... back at the café...here in this village, from this morning...painted before it even happened...it's quite amazing."

"What are you talking about?" Luka snapped.

"I found it...quite by accident...and there I was...in the painting...with you...here... and then they told me who you are...who you *really* are, I mean..." The crazy man was shaking his head, approaching slowly again.

"You see...you're an art dealer...I mean, your disguise...an art dealer...you have ways to get all of the art out...not just mine, it's so unbelievable...just wait till you see...and then my painting could be finished...and yours too...no more need to hide for you...you see?"

In that jumble of words, Luka could see the last four years of his life unraveling. How this insane man knew what he did, who Luka was, and worse that he was under cover, a spy—Luka's mind was racing in panic. He had somehow been discovered, but how, especially like this, by this ridiculous man?

Luka looked around in desperation, not sure what to do next.

"No need to stay here, yes?...you can go home...I can't stay any longer anyway." As he continued forward, Luka realized that this outrageous man would not stop his rantings about Luka's life, even in custody. Claudia, and now the boy on the porch; people would have heard enough, there would be talk, and questions. Questions that eventually would lead to inquiries.

The crazy man was close enough now that Luka could see in his eyes something else, a glazed look that said this man was struggling to maintain, and his hobble had turned into a stagger. He appeared to be on the verge of collapse, but he continued forward.

"We can both...leave this god...forsaken..." and as he reached out to Luka, the man's eyes rolled upwards, and then he collapsed, as if some unseen puppet master had swiftly sliced the strings suspending a marionette. He seemed to crumple in slow motion, striking the alley first with his shoulder; and then with a soft sickening thud, the man's head struck the cobblestones.

Luka stood, stunned for a moment. From the corner of his eye he could see more movement back up the alleyway. The boy and now an old man were standing on the balcony, talking and pointing. Over his shoulder in the distance he could hear footsteps and a woman yelling. He recognized Claudia's voice; she must have summoned a constable. He wouldn't have much time.

Luka dropped to his knees and began quickly searching the man's coat and pants. Blood was now running from a gash on his forehead. Luka felt odd shapes that he couldn't identify. The approaching footsteps grew closer. That was a pocket knife possibly, lumps of something small and soft—maybe berries or nuts?

He reached for the ruddy-white drawbag to peer inside; pencils, a pen, and a handful of notebooks. Across the front of the topmost one he found scrawled the name Erik Richtmulle. Luka quickly stuffed it out of sight, down the back of his trousers, and put the rest back into the little bag.

At that moment footsteps rounded from the street into the alleyway: Claudia and two constables. She stood at the entrance to the alley shrieking into her hands at the scene before her. Luka grabbed the man's shoulders and wailed "Erik, Erik, oh my God," and turned back to the constables. "HELP ME! He's hit his head!"

Chapter 2

Commotion filled the alleyway. One constable managed to quickly fetch a local doctor from just off the square. Luka knew the doctor by name, Dietr, but didn't know him well. He had a reputation for being dour and short, quiet and direct. He arrived looking particularly put-out to be disturbed from his morning routine, even when it was to tend to an unconscious crazy clown man in his local streets.

Luka spoke deep concern to all assembled for Erik, his friend, the man in the checkered hunting coat. Yes, Erik; they had grown up together in Leipzig. Luka hadn't been certain at first, he was so haggard and thin, and unkempt with his growth of beard. But, Luka had finally recognized him as they ran into the alley; this was most certainly Erik. He had gone off to service in the war, but then as they were talking he had suddenly collapsed and struck his head. He repeated the story to Claudia, to the constables, to the boy witness and his father, and now to the doctor, intent on making sure one consistent story would be spread as the story was repeated throughout the town.

As the constables spilled the meager contents of the odd man's bag on the ground and rummaged through them for clues, the doctor pulled Luka aside into a discrete doorway. He spoke quietly, but severely. "Herr Meiter, your friend badly needs medical attention. He most certainly has a concussion, and possibly a skull fracture. But if he goes to hospital..." he trailed off, expecting Luka to follow his meaning.

And Luka did follow. The crazy man was likely a deserter, a former soldier. Even dressed as he was in the checkered-coat, the pants and boots were standard army issue. The hospitals were filled with army wounded; more and more arriving daily, heroes of the fatherland. The checkered madman would quickly disappear, to be interrogated, and then disposed of by an SS officer.

Luka reached into his trousers and produced two one-hundred mark bills and surreptitiously offered them to the doctor. "If there was somewhere else you could tend to him. Perhaps somewhere quietly away...here in town?"

The doctor stared straight at Luka, not reaching for the bills, and letting the awkwardness of his pause underscore the moment. "Herr Meiter. I know who you are, we all know who you are, an art smuggler. Clearly you know important people in the Reich or you wouldn't have so much money at your disposal, or be able to smuggle confiscated war property for a living, or tend to deserters." He paused again to let his distain drip over the conversation.

Luka didn't acknowledge the jabs at his character, still secretly offering the money. "I appreciate your discretion, doctor. I'm simply trying to help an old friend. Nothing more."

The silence continued.

"For your trouble then, yes?" Luka, reached the money out and placed it in the doctor's palm, then closed the doctor's hand around it and withdrew. He glanced down to give the doctor some satisfaction at his arrogance.

The doctor slipped the money into his trousers pocket but continued to stare at Luka. "I can tend to him in the boardinghouse next door to my office, but only for a day at most. Anything more and I risk…"

"Yes, yes. I understand," Luka interrupted. "A few days at most. Thank you so much, doctor."

The ambulance arrived, and the orderlies gathered the crazy man and his belongings together and whisked them into the back. Doctor Dietr announced so all could hear that they would be taking the man to hospital, with the doctor riding in attendance. The crazy man's condition was grave, and they likely would not even arrive in time.

Chapter 3

Luka had planned to spend the remainder of the morning studying for his impending reconnaissance mission out on the notch. Now locked away in the confines of his apartment, he couldn't stay focused. His attention continually drifted back to the composition notebook he had taken from the crazy man, lying on the table among the notated maps and decoded orders. He kept alternating between nervously peering through the corner of the drawn curtains and staring at the journal. Two hours had passed since he had arrived home, and he still had the nagging feeling that the police, or worse, might come banging at his door, wanting to question him about his "friend" Erik from the square.

He would also have to visit the doctor today, to make sure that Erik was somewhere safely out of sight and that the doctor was quiet and satisfied. But what he needed most was to be ready to head out on his mission tonight, prepared for at least two days' surveillance. "Shit!" he cursed aloud, slamming his fist on the window sill. He needed to prepare, but he couldn't ignore the nagging urgency to understand who this crazy man was, and how he could possibly know so much about Luka.

Luka glanced back to the notebook. It was well worn, with a loose back that had swollen from weeks of carrying and constant use; dog-eared corners, dirt smudged front and back. This notebook had been loved over and over again by its owner. Luka glanced back out at the street from the corner of the curtains and convinced himself that no one was coming to interrogate him.

Disregarding the logic of preparation, he walked to the table and picked up the notebook. He flipped the pages through and found that the majority were filled, the last quarter of the notebook still empty. Neat, fluid penmanship inscribed page after page. He opened to the beginning and found written on the inside cover:

Erik Richtmulle
Journal 12
April 1944

If I should be found dead,
please send this to my mother,
Terra Richtmulle,
23 Kohlnstrasse, Frankfurt-am-Main

I love you mama.
I'm sorry we didn't have more time.

The first page began:

April 10 – We lost the battle at Strasbourg. Twenty days of mortar shelling from our heavy artillery, and we were still pushed back three different times. Made our final stand just over the bridge at Kehl. We held it for four days but finally had to evacuate. We blew the bridge before we left, though; that should at least buy us some time to regroup. Now we're headed back to Stuttgart for reinforcements.

The best thing about getting pulled out, we finally got our mail drop, and I have three letters from Helga! It had been weeks since I last received mail. She talks about the clinic at Frankfurt, and how she's training with a nurse there; her new boyfriend and how he can't wait to enlist as soon as he turns eighteen. She is so proud of me fighting for the Fatherland. She retells the evening radio reports of our victories in the Rhein, and she imagines me killing evil Russians, English, and Americans.

I write back, but I don't have the heart to tell her we've just been pushed back into Germany from across the border. How we're losing more men and more ground daily. How the war will be over soon, but not the way she thinks. I'll be dead and Germany will be defeated.

But she also doesn't have the heart to tell me any details about mama's condition, so we go on writing nice letters back and forth. She tells me mama is slowly getting better, but it's what she doesn't say that scares me most. I wish I were back home. We have already lost this war. At home I could help; here I'm accomplishing nothing!

April 15 – Reached the Rhein Valley today, after two days of marching in the rain into the foothills. We were ferried by trucks from Stuttgart as far as Freudenstadt, camped there and restocked. Supposed to join the Third Infantry battalion and move into new positions lining the hillsides, but neither the battalion nor the transports showed after two days of waiting. Captain Vassat was furious, ranting on about the lack of coordination. "This is no way to win a war!" he loves to yell these days. Makes me laugh—here we are pushed all the way back inside our own border and he still believes we'll win the war. Of course I laugh only on the inside!

Now that Heisse and I are dug in, things are better. Our battalion was ordered to dig foxholes on the lower ridge, two to a hole. Advance scouts report no sign of the enemy yet, so cook was allowed to have a fire and prepare a hot dinner for a change. We even had a little warm tea with chunks of hot sugared butter for dessert, such luxury!

We're spread far apart, guarding the valley road below, we have so few men these days. Mostly I only get to see and talk to Heisse. When the Allies come in from France, this is certainly one of the valleys they'll use.

Heisse is describing his daughter to me again, and imagining her first steps, re-reading the January letter from his wife for the hundredth damned time! He keeps apologizing to me for being so boring, but then we quietly laugh like idiots. I really don't mind; it keeps a little hope in me that we might get out of this alive and go home together.

April 21 – Cold today, it's rained for two days straight. The replacement gloves I grabbed in Stuttgart have holes, and Heisse's boots have a tear in the seam. Even though it's late April the nights are very cold here in the hills.

It's against regulations, but Heisse and I keep a small fire lit in the bottom of our foxhole. The Lieutenant walked right by us the other day, he was out smoking his pipe, so very quietly, I didn't hear him until he was above us looking down. He just smiled and continued on. He's a good man; I think he knows there's no hope here, even though he can't say it.

Late in the evening I finally hear the rumbling of heavy machinery coming from the south. It won't be long now.

April 23 – We've been taken by surprise, an artillery barrage from the southwest. It began at dusk and continued all night. We were set to sneak attack the tanks coming up the road, but the Americans are shelling our positions first. They knew we were here waiting.

Heisse and I are dug in well, safe so far, but sometimes we hear screams coming from the opposite ridge as their positions are hit. This is madness—Captain Vassat broke radio silence and called in for air support, but it hasn't arrived. It's just a matter of time until that one unlucky shell finds us.

Heisse actually whispered to me today that he wants to desert. I couldn't believe it! They can shoot you on sight for such talk. But we've grown too close. I would never turn him in, of course, and he knows that. And to be honest, I'm wondering if it's not such a crazy idea. Take our chances in the woods, head west along the ridge, travel by night. If we had enough rations, who knows? Heisse says he overheard the Lieutenant and Captain discussing our positions, and the Nekar Road is close, and the patrols are thin, it's too soft and boggy from the spring rains for trucks. He thinks we could parallel it and stay out of sight. And then what—surrender once we reach a town?

Luka paused from reading. So this was his mad "friend," Erik Richtmulle, son to Terra, brother to Helga, friend to Heisse. A good German soldier doing his duty, slogging his way through the mud and blood, fighting against the Allies, headed toward certain defeat.

Chapter 4

Luka entered Doctor Dietr's office late in the afternoon. The little door-mounted bell's jingle quickly summoned the doctor's young assistant, who greeted Luka cautiously. "May I help you"?

"Yes, I'm here to see the doctor, please," Luka cheerily replied.

"One minute," she answered and quickly retreated.

Luka glanced around the reception area. It was more home than office, with nondescript pictures of flowers adorning fanciful but faded wallpaper. A woman's attention to decoration, pretty and formal, while remaining common and unimposing. Luka expected the doctor and his family must live above the office, quietly attending to the needs of the village, staying cleanly out of unwanted attention's way.

"Herr Meiter," the doctor snapped from the doorway. He turned without waiting for an answer, and called out, "Maurie, I have some business in back, I'm not to be disturbed."

"Yes papa," came her reply.

Dietr led Luka down a long hallway past empty examining rooms and into a back supply area, saying nothing. He shut the door behind them and proceeded through another door that led onto the alleyway. He walked quickly next door into the back of the neighboring house, looking up and down the alley cautiously. The doctor spoke in low tones once they were inside.

"This boardinghouse has been abandoned for a couple of months now. I don't know when the owner will return, if ever. But it's the only option I have for you at the moment."

"Thank you, doctor," Luka replied, "for all your trouble."

The doctor led them both through the darkened house, up the staircase onto the second floor. In a small bedroom just off the landing they reached Erik, lying quietly asleep in bed. The room was flooded with a saffron glow illuminated by the daylight filtering through the drawn brown curtains. The doctor picked up a kerosene lamp from a small table next to the bed and lit it, introducing clarity and detail to the bedroom.

"Erik..." Luka touched the crazy man's arm in mock concern, and shook him gently, as if to wake him.

"Your friend is sedated," the doctor answered. "He's suffered a blow to the head. I would dearly like to see an x-ray of his skull, but I don't risk taking him to hospital. I can feel no fracture, most likely it's a concussion. The best I can do is to keep him still and sedated for the next twenty-four hours and see if any adverse symptoms arise."

The doctor opened one of Erik's eyes and lifted the lamp to it; the pupil dilated in response. "Good. No signs of swelling so far. We'll just have to see. He also took a nasty blow to the shoulder." Doctor Dietr pulled back the blankets to expose Erik's left shoulder. It was covered in bandages that were tinged with blood. Around the edges of the bandage Luka could see the shoulder was swollen and bright red.

"His shoulder was dislocated. I've popped it back in place. It'll be very sore when he wakes, but he's actually quite lucky. The dislocation probably prevented his shoulder from being shattered, and then again—he would have to be in hospital."

"He also has a badly infected wound on his leg that..." the doctor trailed off.

"Yes, doctor?"

Dietr reached down and pulled the covers away from Erik, then pulled back the tape and gauze to expose the wound on Erik's left leg to inspection.

"Well..." he continued. "It's odd. It's clearly a shrapnel wound, likely from an explosion. There's burn marks around the periphery."

Luka could clearly see the black burned flesh that striated the open wound.

"It's several days old, perhaps even weeks. I can't be sure."

The doctor paused again, then looked back at Luka.

"But the odd thing is, this wound has been cleaned and dressed very recently." He looked back and began replacing the dressing and tape. "But it was only a superficial cleaning. I've cleaned it out thoroughly now," he added with a stamp of satisfaction.

"But I believe it already has a bad infection. It's possible the infection has reached his bloodstream, or maybe the bone. We'll have to see how he is once he wakes. And whether he can walk or not."

The doctor roughly replaced the covers.

Luka reached into his pocket and produced another one-hundred mark note and handed it to the doctor. "I thank you again for all you're doing for Erik, doctor"

This time the doctor took the money without hesitation. "Now listen closely," he emphasized. "This place is abandoned for now, but if your friend is found here, there will be no question as to who brought him here. And I will NOT jeopardize my family or my practice for a deserter and his smuggler friend. As soon as he's conscious, he's out of here!"

"Yes, doctor. I understand completely," Luka answered. "And he's sedated?" Luka confirmed.

"Yes, I've given him a heavy dose of morphine so that he'll rest and the swelling can subside a bit. But that's just for today."

"I'll leave the lantern here. There's empty rooms down the hallway if you want to sleep here tonight. You must always leave the curtains drawn, and do NOT use the lantern at night. It must look like no one is here. Come and go through the alley only, the front is padlocked; and you're not to come to my office again. Leave me a note here if you must. I'll check on him again in the morning."

Chapter 5

Alone, held by the quiet stillness of night, hidden in the granite notch on the ridge, Luka watched the moon rise to the east, cresting the opposite side of the valley. He could still hear the low rumble of generators below in the valley; the pedal tone hum told him exactly where the German artillery encampment lay below. Soon he would be able to see it in the rising moonlight.

Usually by now Luka had already slept some, but he wasn't sure he had dozed at all the last few hours when he tried to nap. The morning's events replayed over and over in his mind: the ranting checkered-coated man leaning against the church, then hobbling into the square. Luka abruptly standing at the realization that he was the target of the crazy man's advance. Claudia dropping the plate, Luka running away, first into the street, then down the alley. The crazy man pursuing him, talking endlessly; and then Luka couldn't shut him up, louder now, the things he revealed. "You're a spy, you're not German, you're not really an art dealer, not even a smuggler"—his cover identities peeled back, one by one. Luka's heart pounded in his chest, looking around to see who was hearing this admonishment that the fanatical man was uncovering for the town to hear.

"NO!" Luka's shout woke him with a sudden start, panting, huddled in the cool granite notch. His own voice still ringing in his ears, Luka gritted his teeth at his mistake and concentrated, listening for any response that might come from the camp. Back in training, recruits were required to sleep in front of the class, just to see who could handle the pressure, quietly, with no noise, no snoring, no talking in your sleep. Anyone that slipped up was out, immediately, no second chances.

The moon was high above the opposite hillside, hiding behind a thin meandering strip of cumulus. "Shit!" he whispered to himself, he had missed moonrise, and a clear hour of light between the horizon and the clouds. The moon would be obscured on and off now as clouds passed by through the rest of the night. Luka shook himself, trying to throw off the lingering insanity of the morning, the danger that it potentially represented to him. He was deep in the field, he needed to concentrate. FOCUS, he berated himself mentally, GET TO WORK!

In the shaded moonlight, through his binoculars, Luka could trace the borders of the encampment. It was much larger than the briefing notes had suggested; they were massing for an assault from the southeast. Jack's notes didn't say where the Allied advance would be coming from, but it wasn't hard to look at the terrain maps and know that most of it would have to come up the highway that cut through the Rhein Valley running northwest. All the air drops and paratroopers couldn't cover the basic fact that this was one of the only ways in for heavy tanks from the south. Luka's missions in the last six weeks had all been scattered throughout the Rhein valley. But this was more men and equipment than Luka had expected to see this far east. The only roads leading south out of the valley were dirt, and the Germans couldn't cross the ridges west with their artillery and tanks.

"I'm sorry...you see...I need your help...as an art dealer." Erik's voice echoed in his head again. Luka tried to concentrate and focus through the binoculars. Count the troop carriers on the perimeter of the camp, that was always the first piece of data to assess. Twenty-five men to a carrier, one, two, three, four...

"You can get...my painting for me...it's most incredible...unbelievable, I know...please let me explain."

CONCENTRATE—Luka reprimanded himself. He had lost count again. Alright, forget counting, what else? There wasn't enough light to make out tank types at this distance. He could clearly see the canvas-covered troop trucks in back, but concentration or no, that's all the detail the shrouded moonlight would allow. He would have to wait for morning, and that would mean staying through into the next night before he could leave—he couldn't move by day, too risky. But would Erik be awake by then? Spewing out more rantings to whoever might listen?

Luka pulled out his map, flattened it against the rock, and aligned his compass with the compass rose. In the moonlight he began searching again for the terrain landmarks on the opposite hill. He was sure he was in the right position, he had immediately found the granite notch, but it never hurt to double-check, especially with the size of the encampment he had discovered. First thing to do if you find something unexpected, double-check, triple-check your position; Jack had taught him well, it never hurts to recheck your position.

"You see...it's my painting...and you're in it...this exact scene...in this village...painted before it even happened...it's quite amazing." What the hell could that mean? Luka asked himself.

He turned over the pieces of the morning again in his head, trying to find the truth in them. The most logical explanation was the man was crazy. None of what he said about art and "his painting" and the square made any sense. The constant laughing, his completely disheveled look, checkered hunting coat, an army deserter. He was crazy, delirious, finally deciding to come into a town, any town, after wandering the back forests for weeks.

But then there were the facts the crazy man knew. "I know who you are...You are Luka Meiter, yes?...from Trier...but you're really not German...you're a spy." He tossed his knowledge out to Luka so matter-of-fact, not irrationally, just revealing what he knew. But for what purpose? "You're an art dealer...your cover...an art dealer...you have ways to get all of the art out... no more need to hide for you." The man might be crazy, but he knew things that only a handful of other people did. Had he been exposed?

Luka's heart began to pound again. Somehow, he had been discovered, but surely not by some crazy army deserter. If the Nazis knew he was a spy, he would already have been captured, and would have been tortured and dead by now.

Why didn't the facts add up to an answer? "I wish I had brought the journal!" Luka thought to himself for the hundredth time that night. But the correct decision had clearly been to leave it behind in his apartment. He couldn't spend the night reading the journal out here on a mission, he needed to stay sharp, stay focused, get in and get out, keep his mind on what needed to be done, collect the data. And besides, if God forbid he should be caught, the journal would only ensure Erik and the doctor would be dead beside him, once the SS poured into Trier looking for answers.

Luka's focus came back again, staring down at the red circles on the map. His neck was sore from craning his head over. How long had he been crouched like that, absently holding the compass, staring at the map, but elsewhere, deep in thought? Did I fall asleep again?

Luka stood in disgust. Unable to turn off the thoughts in his head, and too nervous to sleep, he had decided to quietly hike downhill, paralleling the camp on the opposite side of the ridge to clear his head and walk the cramps out of his legs.

Halfway down the hillside a deer sprang suddenly from the low pine brush directly in front of his feet and bounded away up the hillside. Luka gasped at the sudden shock, but his heart leapt into his chest when he heard footsteps and muffled voices coming his way.

He dropped immediately to his belly and lay flat in the pine undergrowth as two Nazi scouts walked up not ten meters ahead of where he lay. Luka could see their boots just ahead.

"See, there it goes," one whispered to the other in German.

"Wouldn't you rather have venison stew than the slop we're getting now?"

"That's too far, we can't follow him that far."

"Stop whining," the second man replied, and proceeded after the deer.

The first man whispered a little louder at the second's back as he disappeared into the night, "We're supposed to be on patrol. We can't be this far out."

"Go on back," his partner jeered from out of the darkness. "Pussy!" he added in laughter.

After standing there for a moment, the first man mumbled, "Moron!", then turned and walked slowly back towards the encampment below.

Luka lay quietly for another ten minutes in the brush, making absolutely sure he was clear again. In the darkness his thoughts were a jumble of adrenaline, berating his own carelessness, and fear at the events of the morning, that he had somehow been exposed by a wild army deserter who might now be spilling a steady stream of previously hidden truths.

Morning came slowly to the valley, progressing gradually from deep violet, to azure blue, then to aquamarine, until finally the red-orange crescent of sunrise began to squeeze against the lip of the horizon. Luka had always enjoyed this time of the day while out on recon. Lying in his crevice, he would watch the rest of the world slowly wake, knowing he had been attentively gathering all details from the night before; but this morning he only had a headache and disgust from worry and lack of sleep.

The day arrived chilly, but the valley was clear of fog, and other than a thin spread of low cloud scud there was the promise of a warm, clear day ahead. The camp began to hum with activity early, and before long Luka had uncovered what he had been sent for. This deployment was large, maybe three times the size that he had expected to find, but the extra men and equipment were devoted almost entirely to artillery, trucks, and supporting manpower. There were only a few light fast-track and half-track vehicles; none of the heavier Panzer tanks, or even the lighter Waffen Tiger tanks, anywhere in sight. And there were no additional foot soldiers, just artillery and support troops.

Luka's assessment was that the Germans planned to line the entire east side of the Rhein Valley from here back to the border with artillery for the Allied advance. There were enough men and equipment staged here to cover the east side of the valley all the way to France. Luka ran the math in his head; the deployment would be sparse, but they could manage it.

Luka felt renewed at uncovering a surprise in Nazi operations. That always generated kudos from Jack and headquarters. But just as quickly, his spirits sank, remembering he would have to stay here all day and into the night. Had he found a massive buildup of heavy equipment, he would have come down from the ridge immediately to send an emergency message. While this was a larger buildup than he had expected, it didn't reflect enough urgency to warrant the risk. Coming out now would only represent an even greater hazard of being caught. Jack would want him to stay low, observe all day, gauge manpower and equipment, reinforcements, traffic; then come out under cover of darkness and notify the courier by shortwave radio.

Luka tried to justify the need to leave today; he wanted urgently to get back to Trier and make sure the deserter was still asleep, before anything worse could happen. But the facts here didn't justify leaving, and Luka knew it. He rubbed the dull, aching headache that had started during the early morning hours, and reached in his backpack for the dried oats and oranges he had brought along.

Chapter 6

Luka's original plan had been to observe and record throughout the day, then slip out slowly and quietly, following the top of the ridgeback north; slow and long, staying high up on the crest, safe, able to observe both sides of his escape. Be out of the hills by midnight, back to his car before dawn. Then as daylight broke and curfew lifted, head to the barn to report, and back to Trier and his apartment by evening.

But nagging thoughts of Erik waking up and ranting away haunted him throughout the day, and by evening he could no longer sit and wait. Luka moved from his position of relative safety in the notch early in the evening just after sunset, to the top of the ridge, while the camp was still active; then cut down and through the adjacent valley, moving perpendicular across the meadow, and following the crossroad directly to where his car was hidden.

Luka knew the risk of getting caught by a patrol was much greater following the open road, but in the end the anxiety of getting back to Trier had overridden the caution and sensibility that had been trained into him. He cleared the checkpoint at Ettenheim just before it closed down for overnight curfew.

Back in Trier, he had been watching the boardinghouse and the doctor's office from the alley for over an hour, but had seen no police or guards. A slow relief pulled Luka's demeanor back from the edge of panic. He walked quietly to the rear of the doctor's office facing the alley and tried the door handle; it was locked. He reached into his jacket pocket for the two slim right-angle picks he kept there, crouched low, and went to work on the simple lock. With little effort it gave way and allowed him entry to the supply room he and the doctor had passed through earlier. In the darkness Luka lit his lens–covered night flashlight and began searching. He quickly found what he was looking for, a handful of syringes and two bottles of morphine, slipped them into his jacket pocket and locked the door behind him.

The back door to the boardinghouse was unlocked. Luka entered slowly and cautiously, stopping to listen on the inside landing, and then again at the bottom of the stairs, but he heard nothing in response. He climbed the stairs to the bedroom, and found Erik, still in bed, alone in the dark, exactly as he had seen him last.

Alone with his new friend, Luka snapped on the night flashlight and placed it on the bedside table, casting an eerie blood-red glow across the room. Luka pulled back the blankets and exposed Erik for inspection. The man looked strong, with large, well-defined muscular arms, but his chest was gaunt and thin, his ribs rising and falling visibly as he breathed. He looked like he hadn't eaten in days. Small sores, cuts, and bruises dotted his chest and stomach; he had been outside and exposed to the elements. He looked a strange combination of good sturdy German farmhand, and haggard street-beggar.

Luka replaced Erik's blankets and turned his attention to the corner of the room where his clothes and belongings had been tossed. The doctor had haphazardly cut away his shirt and trousers—they were shredded. He felt in the pockets but found nothing. Between the constables and the doctor, whatever else might have been inside Erik's pockets was gone. The clothes smelled foul and pungent, the odor of a man that hadn't bathed in several days.

Along the still-intact trouser leg, Luka could just make out a faint stripe, slightly darker than the rest of the deep blue material. Held against the flashlight, the fabric revealed sewing holes along both sides of the stripe. Erik had carefully cut away the gold decoration band of his army uniform, a clear mark of the deserter. The boots were tattered and worn, with tears to the seams, and inside were stuffed two filthy socks, but nothing more.

Luka turned his attention to the plaid hunting jacket. Flannel and bigger than this thin man, it was dirty and stained outside, and lined inside with smooth, fine cotton. The coat was most likely stolen. The pockets' only content was a small silver liquor flask. Luka opened it and caught the faint, sweet scent of anisette, likely the property of the former jacket owner as well. Not the preferred drink of a blue-collared army deserter.

The flashlight revealed little more about the contents of the small bag than he'd quickly inspected in the alley. Several pencils and a hand-sharpener, more notebooks, a handkerchief stuffed with a few biscuits and dried jerky.

The one treasure he did uncover lay inside a small thin wooden box: a beautiful black- and gilded gold pump fountain pen and sealed ink well, nearly empty. Luka carefully replaced the contents and box.

He went back to the bed pondering the sum of these contradictions—the fool in the checkered coat who had stalked him through the square. "Damn," he muttered in the darkness, there was nothing else here to inform him of who this man was, and how he knew so much about Luka. He had hurried off the ridge, risking capture, for nothing.

Chapter 7

Luka returned to his apartment just before dawn. Exhausted, he forced himself to first unload his backpack and gather up his most critical secrets: maps, night flashlight, notes, orders; then stowed them in the false wall behind the bathroom medicine cabinet.

The one incriminating item Luka kept out was Erik's journal. He wanted to find more clues to help him uncover the mystery of this man, and was anxious to get back to reading it. But he made the mistake of lying down to close his eyes first, just for five minutes; and sleep quickly took him over.

Luka woke to darkness. At first he was thoroughly confused and disoriented, thinking he was still out on the notch. It took him a few minutes to realize he was in his apartment on top of his bed—and then he glanced at the clock: seven-twenty p.m. He had slept through the entire day!

Luka sighed in frustration. He had missed his chance to radio in, and he had intended to go back to the boardinghouse that afternoon, and make an appearance with the doctor too.

After gathering some bread, sausage, hard-boiled eggs, and cheese to satisfy his growling stomach, Luka settled into his reading chair in the sitting room with Erik's journal:

April 26 – Heisse talks of desertion continually now. I have to keep shushing him for fear that someone will overhear and turn us both in. Three straight days of artillery shelling and Heisse's talk of desertion...I think I'm going mad!

He's been thinking this out for some time before he started talking to me; he has an answer for every contingency I bring up. But then what? Heisse has a wife and daughter to go back to; they would welcome him with open arms. After the war he could even slip away to Austria or Belgium, but could I go home being a deserter? But then again, we're losing this war, when it's all over who's to say what happens after? Maybe it could work.

April 28 – The Lieutenant picked three men to hike to the supply train five kilometers away to pick up rations, Heisse was chosen, so I spent the day alone. Didn't realize how much I would miss him. He talks endlessly either about his wife and daughter or desertion, nothing else. I swear several times I've thought about running him through with my bayonet myself!

I miss mamma and Helga terribly, I'd give anything for a letter right now. I chain smoke the last of my Strengbergs, staring up at the trees. I wanted to save them, smoke one a night, make them last through the month. But I can't help myself. I can't even taste them anymore, but I don't stop!

April 29 – Heisse returned from the restocking mission giddy like a schoolgirl. They found the supply train twelve kilometers back, not where it should have been, and it was chaos, no organization, squads from up and down the Rhein coming back for supplies with no written orders. Soldiers standing around waiting for the Quartermaster and the officers to make up their minds what to do next.

Heisse had snuck an extra knapsack with him and filled it from the supply train during all the confusion before anyone could realize what was happening. Quartermaster tried to shoo him and several others away, but there was too much commotion to stop any of them.

They headed back here along the Nekar road. At one point Heisse told the other two he had to take a dump, and would catch up. He wandered off the road and stashed the extra knapsack in a hollow tree trunk, so that he could recover it later as supply stock for our coming desertion.

He's definitely going to do it! He's actually planning it! I don't know what to do. I want to tell him he's crazy as a loon, but he knows it's not so crazy as staying here. It's just a matter of time before the tanks roll and we retreat again, or worse, we die here.

May 1 — Gray skies this morning, rain started falling around noon; dirty, sooty rain. It's as if the sky is bleeding out a silent leaden prayer onto us.

Our positions were shelled all last night and all day, concentrated on this side of the valley now. We could hear positions being hit; men screaming in shock and pain, then crying out "Help me," then silence.

Mid-afternoon — without a word Heisse climbs out of our foxhole and disappears. He's probably gone for good, tired of waiting for me to make up my mind. He's finally left. Unbelievable he left in the middle of the day, after all of his careful planning. I keep listening for the single gunshot that will tell me he's been discovered.

In between the shells I can hear the rumble of tanks from the south. They stop just outside the valley before darkness falls. But they'll be rolling again by first light, and the battle will finally arrive.

Suddenly in the haze of twilight, Heisse jumps back into the foxhole nearly on top of me. I almost shoot him, it scares me so badly. He has an enormous grin across his face. He's been crawling around the other foxholes, and taking the dead men's rations when he finds a hole that's hit. I swear he's lost his mind!

Heisse just keeps smirking and cradling his gun in his arms. He's talking to me, but he's staring back up the ridge. "I'm going tonight. It's time. I'm not staying here to be massacred," he says to me in low tones. "Come with me if you want, or don't...but I'm going." He rocks back and forth, staring away, with that incessant grin.

"You're crazy!" I tell him. "Even if we could sneak away, how the hell are you ever going to find your stash of provisions, huh?"

"EASY!" he snaps back at me. "The notch at the bottom of the lone cedar, just off the open glen. It's right where the road joins from Ettenheim, there's a big open meadow shaped like a V there where the roads meet." He pauses, then sneers at me, "Crap, don't come if you want to stay here. But I've got this worked out. We can make it!"

My heart is pounding in my chest now. It should be pounding from the nonstop artillery and the rumbling of tanks, but it's pounding because I know it's time to make up my mind, do I go with him or not?

At one point during the night Heisse is mumbling something to himself, staring off in the distance. "What?" I shout at him over the shelling, but he won't answer me. I sit up and move closer to him and he's repeating over and over, "The notch at the bottom of the lone cedar, just off the open glen. The notch at the bottom of the lone cedar, just off the open glen..."

"Heisse," I try and interrupt him, and tap him on the shoulder. He turns to look at me, but doesn't stop..."The notch at the bottom of the lone cedar, just off the open glen..."

I sit back down, still staring at him. Not sure what else to say.

May 2 – Late in the evening the shelling moves to the opposite ridge, and I'm able to sleep for a bit, I'm not sure how long. As I wake, I turn my head expecting to be alone, but there's Heisse still sitting there clutching his gun. It's very dark. He has the picture out of his wife and baby now, he's smiling back at the little girl in the photograph, even though he surely can't see it.

Then suddenly the world shatters into blinding white light and a shockwave of sound, the force of it violently shoves me onto my back and steals my breath. I'm fighting to stay awake, but my vision keeps drifting out of focus. There is a deafening ringing in my ears, it's all I can hear, and I'm staring through a tunnel of black at the trees reaching up into the darkness.

I start to hear a faint screaming over the ringing in my ears that won't stop. Someone close by is hurt, it must be Heisse! I need to get up, I need to get up! Slowly, as my consciousness returns I realize my mouth is wide open and I'm the one that's screaming, but I can just barely hear myself. I'm lying on my back in the bottom of the foxhole.

I start to move, but a searing pain shoots through my left leg and up my back. I try to sit up again but the pain won't let me. I lay there instead, breathing deeply, still gathering myself. I slowly scoot backwards against the dirt, the pain isn't quite as bad that way. I scoot backwards until my head finds the wall of the foxhole and I scoot myself a little further until I'm propped up just a bit, and I can see myself. My left pants leg is torn to shreds, and I'm bleeding from a black wound above the knee.

Cautiously I push myself up further with my hands. And I find what remains of Heisse, the lower half of his body opposite me, inside what's left of the foxhole, blown apart. The sight and the pain bring a wave of nausea, and I violently throw up my stomach. Each time I heave, each time I move, the searing pain returns.

I try and focus on the dirt wall to my right, I breathe and breathe, calm down, calm down. I stare at the little rocks, and the tiny roots we tore open and exposed with our shovels, Heisse and I making this oh-so-inadequate shelter in the ground. I slow my breathing and listen, but the ringing in my ears is still loud, and I can't hear anything except more exploding shells. I take a deep breath and yell out "HELP US. WE'VE BEEN HIT!" Its sounds to me like I'm talking underwater, and the effort brings the knife edge of the pain back. But I gather myself and yell again "ERIK AND HEISSE, WE'VE BEEN HIT!"

I'm sweating from the effort, and now my forehead is freezing from the sweat and the cold of the night. I realize my helmet is missing. I don't hear anyone coming, or an answer back to my shouts. "HELP!" I yell out again and again in between the exploding shells, but I realize it's futile. The men still out there in the night are hunkered down, trying to stay alive, listening to the rest of us dying around them, hoping they don't get hit like we've just been.

I stare at the stones and the twigs sticking out of the dirty wall, and as I go to cry out again my throat catches, raspy and sore, and I begin to sob. I can't stop, and I can't shout any more. I cry huge tears that start hot and sting my eyes, then run cold down my face and neck as they hit the night air; I try to make myself stop, but I can't. Mercifully my tears end, but my chest continues to heave in dry sobs, and I fall asleep from exhaustion.

I wake up with my face pressed against the cold dirt wall. I slowly turn and there's still Heisse's legs and torso, torn away from the rest of him. Nothing has changed, no one has come; it's very dark, still raining, shells exploding all around.

I brace myself to move again, I'm going to have to help myself if I'm to live, I can't stay out here exposed all night. My back is sore and hurts, but the sharp pain is coming from my leg. If I push and pull myself with only my arms the pain in my leg is bearable.

I pull myself up enough to be able to see out. There's a crater just ahead where the shell hit and tore the foxhole open on the opposite side. From the corner of my eye I'm sure I'm looking at more of Heisse, torn and scattered into a multitude of pieces, but I don't dare look at them directly. I focus on my breathing, and sink back down into the hole.

Moving slowly I find my gun, my knapsack, my canteen, but try as I might I can't find my overcoat or helmet. I fumble around the rest of the foxhole and locate a few more things; my knife, a waterproof tin of matches. Then methodically, not looking directly, gazing a bit off to the side, I bring myself to check around Heisse's body for my overcoat, but I can't find it anywhere. It was over me, like a blanket, probably blown out into the night.

I find Heisse's rifle and with my knife I unscrew the mounting bolts until I can remove the barrel and I'm left with the wooden stock. With strips of Heisse's pants I tie the rifle stock against my leg so that it's stiff and straight. The pain and effort has left me light-headed and panting, and I doze off again.

I wake to find the shelling has stopped. The rain is still falling, and there's just the faintest hint of light to the east, dawn is coming. And I can hear the deep rumble of tanks far away. The main attack is about to start.

I pull myself up and out of the foxhole and into the mud. The effort brings the pain again, but my splinted left leg holds, and it isn't as severe as before. I stay low on my arms and elbows, dragging my feet behind me, with my gun and knapsack slung across my back.

Not looking directly, I manage enough courage to pull myself over to Heisse's mangled knapsack. It's still slung over an arm and part of his chest. I pull it open and find the little tins of meat, fruit and fish, a few wax and sawdust fire starters, the cache of rations he had managed to pilfer from the dead just the afternoon before. It's meager, but it's all I have. I take all of it and his canteen and stuff them into my knapsack. Heisse's coat has been shredded by the explosion, and I still cannot find my own. I only have my light uniform jacket, but I'm out of time—daylight will be here soon.

I drag myself sideways up the slope, perpendicular to the valley floor below. I focus on the path I'm taking, the shortest way out of the foxholes. If I can clear our positions, perhaps I can then stand and hobble up and away along the ridge. I grit my teeth against the pain, but I'm not going to stop. It suddenly hits me that I should find a way to say goodbye to my friend, but I keep moving.

Then suddenly, on the ground in front of my face, lies the crumpled photograph of Heisse's wife and daughter. It was blown out of his hand and several yards up the trail directly in my path, half buried in the mud. With tears coming again I pick it up, and put it inside my jacket pocket, and continue across the ridge.

"Goodbye Heisse," I whisper.

Chapter 8

Early morning, and Luka sat considering the day ahead. He was a day overdue reporting in, but he also needed to pay a visit to Erik, and let the doctor know he hadn't deserted his crazy friend. Who knew what the doctor was capable of if he decided his patient had been abandoned. That was the more pressing matter.

He was scheduled to be in Albstadt by late this evening. A purchase of confiscated French art from a German captain, but that wouldn't be happening now. The meeting was important; it helped maintain his cover, and the bribes kept the army off of his doorstep. But leaving Erik here in Trier unattended to wake, and begin babbling his stories again with all that he knew, was far too dangerous. It was risky, but for now Luka had to stay in Trier.

He left the warmth of his apartment for the chill of the steel gray morning outside, much like the one he had fallen asleep reading about in Erik's journal the night before. He made the walk across town and through the square encountering no one else out this early. Slipping quietly into the back of the boardinghouse and up to Erik's room, on the night table he found a note scribbled with large handwriting. "No Change. Stopped sedation so he'll wake" it read, terse and to the point, just like the good doctor. He pulled back the covers to find a clean shoulder dressing.

From inside his coat, Luka produced a syringe and one of the morphine bottles. He filled it generously and injected it into Erik's good arm, then he sat down to wait and watch. While he waited he read further:

It takes so much effort, but I drag myself slowly up the hillside looking back periodically to see if I've been spied. If I'm stumbled upon I'll say that I was hit and I'm crawling back to command, I'm lost and delirious.

It's light now, the rattle of the tank tracks shakes the valley as they enter, they're below to my left, and I can hear shouted commands from behind me on the hillside. Then the tanks open up. The blasts are deafening, the concussion presses against my chest, and I stop looking back. I crawl until I find a dry streambed that offers some shelter, and I slowly work my way up to the top of the ridge.

It takes hours of crawling, and pain, and the artillery and tank shells are everywhere. My jacket and pants are filled with mud from dragging myself along the ground, and I'm soaked throughout. I finally reach the top of the ridge and pull myself under a squat, fat evergreen. Underneath, the fallen pine needles are dry. I prop myself against the trunk and hug and warm myself as best I can.

While I rest, I can clearly see the battle in the valley below. I count at least forty-five Allied tanks have quickly proceeded up the valley and flanked both sides of the ridge. Even up here I can feel each tank round compress the air like a battering ram, and then splinter the trees on the hillside into a thousand shards of wood, mud, and blood; pieces of men just like Heisse.

We are fighting back with artillery and rocket-propelled grenades. A few tanks have been hit and sit smoldering, but it's clearly a lost cause. From my vantage point on the ridge I can tell it's only a matter of time and we'll be pulling back yet again.

Luka heard the door below quietly open. He quickly stashed the journal away in his jacket pocket. Then footsteps up the stairs, and Doctor Dietr entered the room.

"Good morning, Doctor," Luka cheerfully offered.

The doctor said nothing in reply, just pulled back the covers and proceeded to listen to Erik's chest and take his pulse.

"You're back," the doctor declared smugly.

"Yes, I apologize, in the craziness of that morning I completely forgot that I had business in

Albstadt," Luka replied. "How is he?" he added in his best worried tone.

After several more moments of silence the doctor finally replied without looking his way. "He should be awake by now, three days. The last time I gave him any drugs was two days ago, morphine for his shoulder injury. His concussion must be worse than I expected. But his pupils are still reactive, and his lungs and heart sound clear. I don't see any other indication of trauma besides his shoulder and the leg wound. But of course I'm working without x-rays, or tests of any kind. I just can't be certain."

The doctor paused, deep in thought, then added, "I'm sorry to say, but we must consider moving him to hospital."

"I'm certain you're doing your best, Doctor," Luka reassured him.

But the doctor only stood pondering his patient, and what to do next. He sighed, "You'll be here today?" he asked, glancing back at Luka.

"Yes, all day. I want to be here when he wakes."

The doctor paused again, "Alright, as long as you'll be here, I'll give him a little more time. He seems to be stable."

And with that decision made, the doctor left the room as abruptly as he had arrived.

Luka watched Erik's chest slowly rise and fall, sleeping restfully under the influence of the morphine. "Yes, I can't have you awake and talking, can I?" he offered. "Not with all that you know."

Chapter 9

May 3 – I sleep off and on under the tree. The battle rages on below.

I've been scanning the horizon in all directions with my binoculars. South following the ridge and directly east I see constant movement, that's the rear of our line, and must be backed up for reinforcements. West is the valley and the Allied positions. They have continued pouring in all day. Due north the ridge gradually drops away to a pass, a river, and a dense forest of birch and aspen that turns northeast. I watch up and down the river for an hour, but I see no movement. Far to the northeast I think I can see the Nekar road that Heisse spoke of. I see no other option.

My light coat is shredded from the explosion, and my left pants leg is torn and frayed below the knee. I take strips of my coat and wrap the wound, and then reset my splint. Then I slowly stand and move my left leg gingerly back and forth; the pain returns, but the edge isn't quite so sharp. I decide I can walk slowly and ever so carefully along the ridge.

I'm terrified of slipping on the wet rocks, but I take my time, check my steps, and over the course of the day I manage to make it along the ridge to the pass, and down to the river. The bank is slick and covered with a carpet of dead black leaves. The forest canopy is thick and tangled with the interlocked branches of trees. The river and the dense foliage drop the temperature at least another ten degrees from the ridge top, and there's a light fog that hangs in the dampness.

I begin walking the bank, following the river downstream. I believe I can make the Nekar road in three days at this pace. It should be untraveled due to the wet spring rains. If it's overrun by the Allies— I guess I'll surrender, and if it's still held by us I'll likely be turned over to the SS and shot for desertion. So I walk; at least the effort warms me.

May 4 – I walk during the evenings and rest during the days. But I can only manage a couple of hours of walking at the most before I'm forced to stop and rest. The moon has been rising in the late evening, staying up through till dawn. The ground is thick with mud and a carpet of dead leaves. I have to walk slowly and cautiously so that I don't slip and fall under my bad leg. Today I wandered too close to the river and fell in a small hole that I didn't see. For a time I thought I had broken my right ankle. That would be the end of me with my wounded left leg and a broken right ankle! My boots are soaked through from the wet and mud.

May 5 – Rained all night long. I am ice-cold and soaked. My exposed left leg is freezing and my wound throbs. I keep checking my map but it's too hard to get a bearing from down in this valley through the rain, and the moon is covered behind the clouds tonight.

May 8 – I think I'm lost! It's all I can do not to panic. I climbed up a ridge at dusk before setting out this evening. I scan up and down the river and check against my sectional map. I thought I knew where I was, but the landmarks aren't making sense. Yesterday I should have reached the clearing where the Nekar road crosses. I could see it from the top of the ridge. I know I'm traveling slowly, but I should have reached it by now. There's a light fog hugging the valley and I can't see any clearing in either direction.

I'm lost!

May 9 – Rained all day. My God, this valley is nothing but a forsaken bog! I went up the ridge at morning to sleep a bit. Tried to find a good juniper to hide under, but everything here is soaked. My feet and hands are numb, I can't stop my teeth chattering. At least the tree was full of berries and I was able to eat those.

I've been rationing the tins from Heisse's knapsack, but now that I'm lost I'm worried how soon it will be before I reach the Nekar and the hidden provisions.

I can't keep my leg splint tied tight enough against my leg—after just a few steps it's loose again and rubs my knee terribly, so today I took it off in frustration. I can walk with my leg straight on my own, and I won't have the rubbing. At least I was able to use it for firewood.

The days are terrible! At night I can concentrate on my walking, but during the day I brood when I can't sleep. What have I done? My life is over. I have nowhere to go. I'm lost! What was I thinking?

After giving Erik another dose of morphine, Luka slipped out of the boardinghouse in the early afternoon. Hiking north out of the village, he soon arrived at the turnoff for the abandoned farm. Following the familiar routine, he walked past the entrance, scanning for any sign of another visitor. Seeing nothing suspicious, he walked up the small rise of a hill, to the parking lot of the little chapel. From here a clear view of the abandoned farm lay below. Crouched in the bushes he waited and watched.

To the south, flashes of white light along the horizon punctuated the dusk. The front was moving closer to the village each day. From the safety of the hill Luka could clearly see the old hay barn doors, askew and haphazard like the rest of the structure, and with his binoculars, he quickly located the first marker—the wooden plank left leaning against the bottom hinge. No one unexpected had been in the barn. Scanning now to the near corner of the forsaken sorghum field, Luka found the other marker that he hoped wouldn't be there, three small stones stacked neatly atop the corner post; the emergency sign the courier had left for him, "contact immediately!" Luka dropped his chin in disgust; the courier had already been there twice and found nothing to pick up. His hope was that the courier had missed a day assuming Luka had stayed out an extra night, but no such luck. The courier would have already reported back to Jack as well: Luka had missed a drop, there was trouble.

It was dark enough now. Luka headed down the hill, across the road, and onto the dirt path crossing through the adjoining field. At the low fence dividing the two farms, he hurdled over and into the rows of scattered wild sorghum stalks and tall unkempt grass and weeds, stopping to knock down the three stones on the fence post.

The old hay barn loomed into view as he walked carefully through the uneven rows, ominous in the darkness. Luka never liked this rendezvous point, the hay barn in the abandoned milk dairy. It was close to town, easy to walk to, and didn't require a risky drive in the night violating curfew. It was inconspicuous and out of sight below the little hillock that held the village—everything you could want in a drop point. But even in daylight the barn had always looked evil and predatory to Luka. Long ago one wall had been knocked off its supports by a heavy windstorm, and now the years and neglect had combined to drag the entire structure down and sideways, until it stood sagging, on the edge of collapse. The odd diagonal lean of the building had stretched the upstairs loft and window openings into grotesque shapes that resembled the mouth and eyes of some malevolent creature, conspiring to collapse in on, and swallow up, anyone that dared enter.

Approaching the doors now, Luka entered the old barn and stopped for a moment to listen in silence. Even though the marker told him he was alone, he had run into an occasional squatter over the years. Most often it was a raccoon or a family of skunks that from time-to-time had surprised him; but once he nearly tripped across two college kids making love in the hay, and another time a drifter had decided to hole up to ride out a cold spell.

Hearing nothing, Luka switched on his red-lens–covered flashlight and made his way through the strewn hay to the back of the barn, and the locked cellar doors. Kneeling down, he twisted the combination into the lock, then opened the doors. He walked down into the dank cellar, closing and locking the doors above him from below.

Safely inside the concrete shelter, he felt along the wall until he found the heavy turn switch, and snapped on the lights. He followed the narrow dirt entryway around a corner and down to a small concrete bunker. Inside were the familiar locker, cots, canned rations, sealed tanks of clean water, rifles and pistols, ammunition. Luka sat down at a desk that held note pads, maps in German and English, a shortwave radio, and transmitter key.

Below the desk sat the old diesel generator, with a vented exhaust leading through the concrete wall and outside. Luka tipped the generator back and listened to the slosh of fuel, at least half a tank. He set the choke lever, and holding firmly to the top, began turning the hand starter crank. The generator sputtered and caught, sending a backfire of smoke into the room as it slowly rose to noisy life. The lights flickered brighter as the battery charged against the generator. It was a warm evening, so Luka set the choke back after only a few seconds, and the generator quieted down into smooth operation.

Luka switched on the shortwave radio, and while he let the vacuum tubes warm up he reviewed again the message he would send tonight. The short broadcast would tell both his courier and Jack that his report was ready for pickup, and hopefully allay any concerns about his being two days overdue:

GREGOR <STOP> RE MATTISSE COLLECTION YOU DESIRE <STOP> LOCATED STRASBOURG WITH ADDITIONS <STOP> SECURED AND

HIDDEN <STOP> 23K MARKS TO
INTERCEPT DELIVERY <STOP> ELSE
DESTINED BERLIN <STOP> LET ME
KNOW SOONEST <STOP> DELAYED
TWO DAYS UNAVOIDABLE <STOP>
MARTIN <END>

Chapter 10

On his way home, Luka slipped back to the boardinghouse to leave a one-hundred mark bill and a note for the doctor, "Erik didn't wake today. I'm very concerned. You're right. I'm arranging transportation to move him out of the village and to a discrete, private hospital. Back in the morning."

At the bunker in the old hay barn he left a detailed report on the Nazi Army deployment along the Rhein, and another note for the courier explaining, "Delayed to Albstadt, two days at most. Unavoidable. Otherwise fine."

Now safely back in his apartment, Luka continued the search for clues to Erik:

May 11 – The wet is constant. Even when it's not raining the trees drip and the forest floor never dries. It smells like rot and fungus all night long as I walk. I climb into the hills during the day to sleep, every now and then I can find some dry pine straw, but most of the time I'm soaked.

My rations are getting low, but I still have a few tins of meat and fruit left. I've been eating juniper berries whenever I can find them, but I think they're giving me diarrhea. The food should hold, provided I can find the Nekar road and Heisse's stash of provisions, but I should have been there already. I have to figure out where I am, fast!

My left leg throbs and smells badly. What else can go wrong?

Tonight while walking I spy a structure across the river. I almost missed it it's so small and dark, tucked back well into the tree line. I sit on a stump watching for the longest time, but I see no movement or light, and finally I cross the stream and approach.

It's a hunting cabin, small and sagging in the center, with a roof that looks to have collapsed on one side. The door has been broken open and now lays askew, exposing the dark interior.

I snap on my flashlight and step inside; the floor creaks and sags as I step across it. Sweeping my flashlight through the darkness, I find a small cook stove and washbasin along the far wall, next to a broken cupboard. Piles of rags, wood, newspaper, and broken glass lie in an odd pile in the corner. The windows have all been broken out and the rain is blowing in.

The other side of the room once held a table and a couple of wooden chairs, but they now lay broken and shattered in a heap. There's a pile of burnt wood and ash smoldering low nearby. Someone's been here recently.

The only other door leads to a small bedroom at the back of the cabin. I sweep my light inside but only find an odd mix of shadows. As I approach the little room I hear something, a sudden shuffle of movement. Maybe I've surprised an animal. With my free hand I reach inside my knapsack and bring out my Luger.

Slowly sweeping my light back and forth I approach the room. At the far end across from the door stands a metal cot, with a shoddy, moth-eaten mattress on top. A small wad of rags and what looks like old clothes lies beside it.

As I step into the room I sweep my light to the right, and out of the corner of my eye I just catch a shadow moving quickly towards me. I instinctively raise my arm in defense, and something strikes my forearm hard. I start to back out of the bedroom, but my bad leg buckles underneath me. My Luger and flashlight go flying, and I hear them clatter to the floor, along with something heavy.

I'm on my back, flailing, my leg and now my arm both searing with pain. As I scramble backwards trying to get out of the doorway, I'm patting the floor, franticly feeling for my pistol. Instead I see my flashlight, still on, pointed askew into the corner, and I grab it quickly.

In the near corner, back pressed against the walls, squats a person, raising an axe with both hands. As my flashlight beam shines across the face, the eyes squint, and blindly the axe comes swinging towards me again, the stroke deliberate and hard. This time I move quickly to the side, against the doorway, and miss the blow as it strikes the floor next to me.

In front of me, in the scattered light, between my legs I spot my Luger. I grab it and point it at the stranger's face and yell "ACHTUNG!"

One hand still on the axe handle, with the free hand the stranger reaches out to grab the top of the handle near the blade. It's a small, smooth hand, too small and out of place to be wielding an axe, a young hand. With some effort my attacker lifts the axe into the air again, ignoring my command.

I raise up onto my knees, and lean forward, my gun pointed inches away from my foe's forehead. "TOTSCHIEBEN" I yell through gritted teeth, and now I point my flashlight quickly to the gun barrel. "I WILL SHOOT YOU DEAD IF YOU MOVE!"

For a moment we are frozen there, the axe raised, my pistol pointed. But the immediate threat seems to have eased, and I begin backing away slowly, until my back reaches the doorway.

Gathering my wits, I sweep my light at my attacker. Dark black eyes meet the beam and squint again. It's a woman, hair matted, face smeared with greasy dirt, but with beautiful high rounded cheeks, and a perfect small nose, and lips drawn into a thin sneer.

In astonishment I lower the Luger, and she raises the axe in threat. I quickly raise the Luger once again, and now I can see the axe shaking. Her bare arms reveal thin rippling muscles and tendons, doing their best to wield the heavy instrument, attempting to look strong and threatening; and I realize I could quickly overpower her, reach over and knock the axe out of her hands, but I let her keep the weapon, her protection for now.

I slowly, cautiously drop the Luger into my lap and then raise my open hand to her; hold it there. In response she raises the axe even higher. She grits her teeth and growls back in defiance, and I say softly "Fine, you keep it. I'm not going to hurt you."

I keep my hand held up, palm out, just in case she tries to swing it again, and finally she lowers it, just enough.

Slowly I sweep my flashlight across her again. She has on a dirty brown cotton skirt that reaches her knees. She has no shoes, and the bottoms of her feet have visible calluses and scabs. Her shirt is a man's dress shirt. Even with the sleeves rolled up into two fat cuffs, they still hang down below her elbows. The tail sits long and ragged on the floor surrounding her.

Playing the light across her face again, she squints and sneers. She clearly does not like submitting to being examined.

And now I can see rivulets of water running down the wall and onto her shirt coming from the rain outside. I shine my flashlight above, and find a gaping hole in the top corner of the room above her.

I lower my flashlight back into the center of the room so she can see me while I still can see her. I smile and wave with my hand, motion for her to come over to me, to get away from the water. She raises the axe again.

"No, no," I try and say gently, "come out of the rain."

I motion again, go to kneel towards her. As I raise up, she sucks in air quickly between her gritted teeth and a look of terror crosses her eyes, like a cornered animal.

I raise my hand again, palm out, a sign of resignation—"alright, alright"— and I slowly sit back down. "Everything's fine".

I settle back against the doorframe and she relaxes, axe still raised, but not as high. I sit for the longest time wondering what to do next. I don't want to leave my flashlight on all night and drain the batteries, but I don't dare turn it off and risk getting struck again. My arm is throbbing from the blow, and I shake it out.

She gasps and raises the axe yet again; any sudden movement of mine makes her jump in reflex.

Outside I can hear birdsong; dawn must not be too far away. I snap my flashlight off, and there is dark blue light filtering through the broken windows. At first the room is dangerously dark and devoid of details, but I sit very still, ready to snap the flashlight back on. As my eyes adjust I can make out her silhouette against the wall, the light beginning to find all the corners of the little room, and I relax again.

May 12 – I rest but don't sleep. Sitting still, we cautiously watch each other until the light of day finally breaks under a constant rain.

I raise my hands again, try to gesture her away from the runoff behind her, but she doesn't budge.

Then I gesture to the far corner, away from me, near the tattered bed, and ask quietly, "How about moving over there?" She slowly looks sideways at where I'm pointing. "Yes, over there," I repeat in as cheery and nonthreatening a tone as I can manage. Where I'm pointing is farther away, less threatening from me, maybe she'll accept that. She glances over again, and back to me, suspicious.

"Just get out of the rain," I say, and reach around and point to my back.

She looks partially over her own shoulder, then back at me. Recognition seems to cross her face.

"Yes, just get out the rain. You must be soaked by now."

She raises up, still watching me carefully, holding the axe across her lap, and slides along the wall to the far corner; then plops back down, back firmly planted against the reassurance of the dry corner.

"Good," I finally say and try to shoot her a smile, but she doesn't respond.

With that small victory, I raise up stiffly. I put both hands out in warning to her, "It's alright, I'm just getting up." I pause, and this time she lets me do so without reacting.

"Good," I say, as I get to my feet. Stiff, now with a painful leg and arm both throbbing. "Maybe we make a little progress?"

Surveying the cabin in the drab light of the rainy day doesn't reveal much better news; it's already been rummaged and ransacked of most usable items. The large hole in the roof starts in the bedroom but crosses and extends into the entry room, and the incessant rain is buckling the wall that's slowly being engulfed in moss.

The tiny kitchen doesn't hold much else. There are a few battered and bent utensils lying around, and I discover a partial sack of dried beans hidden in a broken corner of the cupboard, but they're covered in mold.

The opposite end of the entry where a table and chairs once stood is a pile of partially recognizable furniture that's now been hacked to pieces for firewood. She has built whatever fires she could manage right on the cabin's floor, and very soon this little pit will collapse to expose the earth below.

I walk around inspecting the place closer, looking for anything of use. Each time as I return to the bedroom doorframe she is still there, huddled in the far corner, watching my every move.

The only item that might hold some promise is an old steamer trunk I can see tucked beneath the metal cot, beside her. But I decide better of the effort of retrieving it from under the bed, and scaring her yet again.

With daylight now here, and the danger of the night over, a wave of exhaustion washes over me, and I collapse into a heap on the floor near the pile of broken furniture. I snap off what's left of the cross-pieces of a chair back and pile the wood together over the coals. In the corner is a box of damp matches, and after several tries I finally coax one to light, then manage to ignite the pile of wood scraps.

I prop my back against the wall, clutching the Luger in my hand; the small fire in front of me, and for the first time in over a week I let gratitude wash over me for some shelter from the rain, some warmth, and companionship, as wild and hostile as that might end up being.

Chapter 11

Luka watched a rainy morning dawn over Trier from his drawing room window. Plotting what to do next, he had gotten little sleep the night before. The doctor's patience had certainly been pushed to the limit. Now approaching day five, and coming to the end of the journal, Luka still hadn't discovered the insight into Erik that he had been searching for. He was now two days overdue to Albstadt, and the Captain would have been long gone by now; no point in trying to save that mission. Luka had racked his brain during the night trying to think of a place to hide Erik, and how to transport him there without violating the driving curfew. Then suddenly, the answer dawned on him, simple and elegant.

Back at the boardinghouse now, Luka passed the early morning waiting for the doctor to arrive, continuing through the journal:

May 13 – I wake with a sudden start, and for a moment I don't recognize where I am, and jerk backwards in surprise at the cabin surroundings; but the fresh pain in my arm, and the numbing pain in my leg nudge me back to reality. The little fire on the floor is a sad smoldering pile of damp wood again, unable to completely catch and burn. Through the windows I can see the day is steel gray, and the rain continues outside, unabated.

I stand, stretch, and then peer around the doorway; the woman has fallen asleep in her little corner of the bedroom, the axe handle resting in her lap. She's now wrapped in a long flannel coat, legs tucked up tightly underneath in a fetal ball, maybe a prize she discovered from the trunk under the bed? I take advantage of the daylight and her sleeping, and study her in more detail from the relative safety of the doorway. She has jet-black hair and olive skin, and despite the dirt that cakes her features, beneath I can see hints that she is smooth and soft. Her hands are covered in scars, the look of recent hard physical labor. She reminds me of a gypsy girl Heisse and I watched dance for money in Troyes.

I knock quietly on the doorsill, and she gently opens her soft eyes, the whites clear and large. For a moment she is serene and beautiful, but she quickly recalls where she is and gasps, eyes wide, and tries to back into the corner at the sight of me still occupying the doorway of her little hideout. She clutches again at the axe handle.

I hold out my hands again as a gesture of peace, and then slowly enter the room, crouch down on the floor, and pull the trunk from under the cot, scraping it between the floor and the metal frame as I pull it along, the whole time watching her.

She scrutinizes me intently, wide eyes flicking back and forth from me to the trunk. I free it slowly, continuing to watch her, then drag it into the entry room. The lock is mangled and has been beaten off, probably by her axe. The contents inside are scattered in disarray. Some sheets and rags, shotgun shells, a ramrod, a bottle of gun oil and bottle of cleaning solvent, and a wool flannel hunting jacket, similar to the one she has on. I take it out and try it on. It's definitely a man's, big—too big for me—but the oversized warmth of the wool is welcome.

The rain is beating harder now, and the cabin offers sparse shelter. Rain and wind blow in through multiple gaps and holes. And no matter how many times I coax it, a fire won't stay lit. All the contents of the cabin are saturated. Even when soaked with the cleaning solvent the fire roars quickly to life, then gradually sputters and eventually dies out.

My stomach repeats a loud protest rumble for food, and so I sit down against the wall, open my pack, and sort through what rations I have left. There's three tins of meat, two tins of peaches, a tin each of apples and apricots, and some dry wafers. I line them in front of me on the floor, my dwindling stock of provisions.

I sit pondering my rations, calculating in my head how many days I can last using the little cabin as a base, scouting during the day for the Nekar, and Heisse's cache of supplies. Then I spot her, squatting in the bedroom doorway, eyeing me intently.

I motion with my hand for her to enter, but she doesn't respond, she just keeps watching me. I pat the floor beside me and motion to her again, "Come on." I try and persuade her in, but still no response; it's like trying to coax a frightened animal in beside me. And then I see that she's not watching me; her eyes are firmly fixed to the line of food on the floor at my feet.

I sit for the longest time and then finally sigh in resignation. "God help me," I whisper, and shake my head. I grab a tin of peaches and hold it up in offering.

"Want some?" I try and entice her in again.

She rises on her haunches in anticipation and looks at me with a question in her eyes.

I wave the can of peaches at her again. "It's alright, come on in."

The girl rises quickly. Her face brightens in response, she stands and walks to the middle of the room, hikes her skirt up to her waist, and lies down on the floor. The flannel coat spread wide reveals her dark black pubic hair.

I sit staring in shock and disbelief and she turns her head sideways to look at me, a look of anticipation.

"Oh... no," I start softly, and then repeat louder.

"No." I rise on my good knee and move to her. I reach out to pull her skirt down, and she looks at me quizzically, confused.

"No, no," I repeat. "You don't have to do that."

And now she's tugging at my arm, trying to pull me on top of her. With her free hand she begins unbuttoning her shirt, revealing smooth, small round breasts, and pulls my hand onto her chest.

"NO," I insist louder, and pull her shirt closed.

I take her hand and pull her up from the floor. She clutches at her open clothes in surprise and sits up, watching me with confusion.

"Here," I say, and I reach out and put the can of peaches in her hand. I close her tiny fist around the can and then withdraw back to my corner. I raise the other can of peaches in my own hand and point from me back to her.

"It's alright. That's for you. It's alright."

Sitting half-naked, clothes clutched against her body with one hand, a can of peaches in her other, she speaks for the first time. "Ja jsem takovy hlad."

Her voice is low-pitched and rough, and I don't understand a word of what she's saying, so I only nod. The first other human I've heard in ten days.

"Dekuji," she adds, staring intently at the can of peaches, and then stands and runs to the wash basin.

Dekuji—I think it's Czech for 'thank you', but I'm not entirely certain. Standing at the little broken cupboard, she begins banging furiously at the can with a bent fork.

I stand and walk over to her, grab her hand gripping the useless utensil, and lead her back over to sit by me. I reach into my knapsack, find the little can opener, place her tin of peaches on the floor, and open it for her.

She snatches the can out of my hand before I can reach it to her, and begins digging the sweet contents out from inside with her fingers.

I eat my own peaches slowly, watching her. She's like an animal, crouched on the floor, shirt half-open, breasts exposed hanging beautiful and inviting; vulnerable in her ravaging hunger.

I keep expecting her to cut her fingers in her haste on the open can lid, but she doesn't. My own peaches are like ambrosia, and from time to time she moans in ecstasy at her own little feast.

I open up the tin of meat too, so I can watch her eat that much longer, and then a couple of packets of crackers and water from my canteen.

Then I lay down on the floor, my head resting on my arm, exhausted, as I watch her run her fingers inside each can, making sure any last remains are hers. The whole scene is intensely erotic, but at the same time quite desperate.

I'm watching her through drowsy eyes, as the light of the day is fading outside.

Chapter 12

I wake with a start to a completely dark cabin.

"Hello," I call out gently, but there's no response.

"Hello," I repeat, this time a little louder. And I sit still, holding my breath, listening to my own heartbeat. Only silence answers. There's no warm fire, no light to see at all. She's not here, and my heart sinks.

And then, like a rushing wave...reality floods over me.

Oh God! I pat the floor around me, but I can't find anything recognizable. My backpack, my flashlight that was right in front of me, they're gone!

I feel around and around the floor, but I only find small odds and ends that don't matter, a pencil, a crumpled piece of paper, a stick of broken furniture.

"SHIT!" I shout into the darkness, and my heart is now pounding in my ears.

I push myself back until I reach the wall and force myself to take several calming breaths until I can think. I start over again, patting the floor outward away from me in an arc. I find the little pile of furniture that's now firewood, and just beyond that I feel the fire I tried to light, now cold, wet, and dead. I keep patting, moving the pattern outward in little arcs, and then I touch something flat and smooth; it's my notebook. Oh god, she's been through my knapsack!

I keep up my blind search, patting methodically, spreading out away from where I sit, trying not to panic, and begin slowly finding things. The floor is littered with debris. Something small and flat, crinkled, it's the photo of Heisse's wife and daughter. I collect what I can lay my hands on in front of me on the floor. It's not much. I hold items up to my eyes to try and discern, but I already know the collection is meager.

I pat methodically over and over along the floor until my back is sore from crouching, and I've covered the room more than once; but there's no tins of food, no maps, no flashlight, no pistol; my knapsack and canteen are gone as well.

I locate my notebooks, a few pencils, Heisse's crumpled family photo, that's it. And now I am furious—at the woman, at myself—for being such a fool.

May 13 – I spend a long, sleepless night waiting for morning to arrive so I can finally confirm what I already know to be true: she left, and took nearly everything I had. I let my guard down, and she took complete advantage of me. And now I've sealed my fate.

Part of me secretly hopes she's returning. I make up justifying stories, that maybe she was going for help, or she has another hiding place close by, somewhere safer. But every reason I dream up for her leaving rings hollow and stupid in my ears.

She's gone; she saw an opportunity and took it. The truth of it makes me sick to my stomach. I'm lost deep inside this valley that I don't know, and my chances of finding Heisse's hidden rations have faded to the barest of hopes. With no maps, really it's desperation. But it's the only chance I have to survive.

The rain is endless and seems to leak into every crack of the doomed little shack. But eventually morning arrives, and I am grateful for even a little daylight.

I make a small pile of items to take with me: the hunting jacket, my notebooks, a few pencils, my one good pen that Helga gave me for graduation, the photograph—that's all I have left. Inside a pocket of the hunting jacket I find a small empty hip flask. At some other time I would have found that funny, but not today. Today it just strikes me as appropriate—more useless stuff. I decide to take it anyway.

Using the gun solvent and rags from the trunk, I clean my wound the best I can. It's now red and swollen and painful to the touch. I tear strips of bandages from one of the sheets and rewrap it.

Using what's left of the sheets, I fashion a little makeshift drawbag to store my meager cache of items and tie it to one of my belt loops against my side.

In the evening I'll climb the ridge and try to get my bearings from memory. I have to find the Nekar road now, or I'll certainly die. But right now all I want to do is use the daylight to put some distance between me and this cabin.

I walk through the morning, even though it's dangerous. Part of me half hopes that I'll meet her walking through the dank little valley ahead of me. And then what? Would I try to kill her to get the rations back? She has my gun, and knife, and I'm sure she's not afraid to use them.

I walk until evening, then climb the ridge to my right. My stomach has been growling all day, and now it's cramping.

At the top of the ridge I scan around me, but nothing is familiar. In the gray overcast I can't see any stars and am not even sure which way north is! I try hard to recall the details from the maps I'd reviewed so many times, but right now I can't remember them. I do remember the bald ridge knob to the west of the battlefield, it was easy to pick out on clear days. I remember it clearly marked on the map too; maybe I can see that. I scan the horizon, squinting into the distance, but I can't see anything I recognize. I circle and circle in panic, trying to find that one landmark, but it's no use.

I slump to the ground in tears, I'm more lost that I was even before I found the shack, and I'm more than likely dead. My head is now light with hunger and thirst. I bend down further and press my lips against the crevasses of the rocks on the ridge and try and suck up what rainwater still sits in the deep cracks.

I wake to a dry morning. Broken clouds cover the sky from horizon to horizon, promising more rain for the coming day. I lay with my head against the stones and realize my stomach has stopped protesting against the lack of food. How odd, I think to myself, that doesn't make any sense. It's been at least forty-eight hours since I've eaten anything. My body seems oddly calm, until I finally decide to sit up, and suddenly I'm faint.

I fight through the dizziness, trying to focus, and prop my back against a nearby stone and take in several deep breaths. My lips are dry and cracked, I'm thirsty again, and I remember last night, scanning and scanning the horizon.

I'm not even sure what day it is any longer, but in the daylight I resume my scanning for the knob hill that I can recall from my maps. I look and look in all directions, but still can't find the landmark. I finally give up, sighing in resignation, staring into my lap. I think I should get up and walk, but now I *can't remember why—oh yes, the Nekar, and Heisse's stash of rations. That's certainly worth getting up for, but somehow, sitting here seems much easier. I'll just sit for a while, I think.*

I wake again with a start. I'm still propped against the stone rock. My neck aches from falling to one side, and my butt is sore and has fallen asleep from the hard ground. I try slowly to stand, but my legs refuse to cooperate. Over and over I try, but the best I can manage is to get to my knees. I kneel, panting, catching my breath and trying to clear my head. As I wait to recover, I gradually realize that I'm gazing right at a dirt road far ahead in the next valley.

I finally manage to pull myself to my feet, and look again. I was concentrating so hard on finding the bald knob, I hadn't even been able to see the little dirt road in the distance. I shake my head and try to focus.

Away, much farther down the little dirt road, I think I can see something flickering, but it's hard to be sure. I could be imagining a town ahead ahead, I don't know. But I'm going down the other valley, down that road and what lays beyond. I'm sure it's not the Nekar, but I have no other choice.

This valley is easier to walk in. The first night I walk on the road, but once I'm surprised by a convoy of army trucks. In my own foggy haze, I didn't even realize what I was seeing was headlights in the distance, coming at me. I had to dive for the meadow at the last second as they rounded a curve. Now I walk in the meadow just off the road.

I haven't eaten anything for three days now, and I've grown so weak. I have to stop constantly and gather my strength. Thankfully there's standing water everywhere from the persistent rains, at least I'm able to drink.

"The notch at the bottom of the lone cedar, just off the open glen. The notch at the bottom of the lone cedar, just off the open glen. The notch at the bottom of the lone cedar…"

"I KNOW, HEISSE! I heard you the first damned time! What do you think I'm looking for out here? It should be right here."

And then I trip across a rock, nearly landing in the dirt face first. Oh my God, I was wandering in a daze, headed away from the road. I thought I was talking to Heisse. We had found the Nekar and were looking for the stash of food. Was I actually talking to him out loud? I'm not sure…

As I round a bend in the road I can see the lights of a small village far ahead. I squint and squint, standing in the middle of the road, trying to clear the hallucination away, but it's real. The lights remain; I'm sure it's a town. I walk slowly and cautiously but see no people or traffic on the road. Ahead there is a dirt turnoff that climbs a small hill.

I take the turnoff so that I can scan the village better. Maybe I can break into a cellar of one of the houses.

It seems like it takes me an hour, and I have to stop over and over to catch my breath. I reach the top of the hill exhausted.

The dirt turnoff continues down the lee side of the hill, gradually meandering until ending at a lone building on the edge of the forest overlooking the village. The building is long and thin, like a warehouse. It's lighted and surrounded by a chain-link fence.

I wander down the road slowly. As I approach the fence I can hear voices. I crouch low and listen, but I can't make out what they're saying, and I can't see them. I think it's two men standing outside on the opposite side of the building.

A car starts, I hear a gate open, and the car drives away crunching the gravel beneath it, headed towards the village below. As it speeds away I hear the gate close, then footsteps walking back in the gravel. A metal door opens and shuts, and then all I hear is the rain. I stay low and quiet for a long time, making sure there is no one else.

Hearing the back door open, Luka hid the journal in his jacket. Doctor Dietr climbed the stairs and stopped at the bedroom doorway, stunned. Erik was gone, the bedding neatly folded and stacked on the floor beside where Luka now sat.

"Good morning, Doctor," Luka greeted him. "I wanted to make sure and thank you for all your wonderful care myself. I folded the…"

"Where is he?" the doctor blurted.

"I had him moved during the night."

"Impossible!" the doctor scoffed.

"Oh no," Luka smirked, "not for my friends." The doctor stared back in disbelief, a scowl across his brow.

"I never heard a thing! How?"

"Well…my friends are very good at getting in and out of places quietly." Luka paused to let that point sink in. "Erik is now safely being cared for. At a…private facility."

"Where?" the doctor demanded.

"Doctor," Luka paused, "isn't it better if you don't know, hmmm?" The doctor looked back without answering. Luka stood and offered him a small envelope.

"Three hundred marks more inside. Please take it with my deepest gratitude." The doctor slowly reached for the envelope, as if in a daze, but Luka didn't let go. The doctor looked up at him.

"And also, for your discretion…yes?" Then Luka let go of the envelope.

The doctor turned in an indignant huff and stomped down the stairs.

"Of course…" the doctor growled back as he left, slamming the door behind him.

Luka grinned. His veiled references to smugglers and the bribes had created the desired effect. The doctor surely wouldn't talk now; he was in too deep. And he had stomped out just as Luka had hoped for.

Luka followed the stairs down to the main landing, walked to the end of the hall, and then continued down the stairs leading to the stone cellar, where Erik lay sleeping.

"Now that he's been taken care of…" Luka spoke aloud to Erik. Then he sat down in a folding chair beside the lamp to make sure the doctor didn't return, and to finish the journal:

I'm shaking and my teeth are chattering from the cold. I'm dizzy, thirsty, and starving. In the distance to the east the glow of sunrise is on the horizon. Far below I can see early activity in the town. A man is loading boxes into the trunk of a car. I can't go down there now, I'll hide in the warehouse for tonight.

I cover the fence with my coat and climb over, it takes me several attempts, and I have to concentrate to keep my feet from slipping as I climb. I land on the far side in the grass, panting from the exertion. Outside the building is empty, wooden boxes and crates stacked randomly, but I can see no indication of what could be inside.

I step softly towards the back of the warehouse away from the lights. The building is battered and pock-marked from gunfire. I find no entrance in the rear, but there are a row of roll-up delivery doors. They are all locked, but one is dented in on the side about halfway up. I put my weight into it, and the door groans and gives a bit. Soon I can wedge my leg, and then my waist, and my chest and arms through. The door creaks in protest, and I cringe at the noise. I push myself into the crack more until the door finally gives enough, and I fall through to the concrete floor inside.

I sit and listen for several minutes, panting again, trying to gather myself. I hear nothing in response to the noise of the door, only the constant patter of the rain.

I'm sitting behind stacks and stacks of large flat panels leaning against a wall that stretches out in opposite directions away from me. Their leaning leaves a small low crawlway against the floor that I follow along the wall. I crawl until I reach a door against the cinder block wall and open it. It's a utility closet, with power lines and water pipes running from floor to ceiling.

I quietly close the door and lay my head down in the darkness, wet and cold, but grateful to be out of the rain and the constant walking, and pass out from exhaustion.

Chapter 13

I'm jolted awake by a nightmare. I'm falling down a concrete shaft. I can hear voices, they're far away and echoing. For a time I lay in the dark on the hard floor, disoriented and trying to remember where I am. My heart is pounding, but then I finally remember the little closet and how I came to be here.

Did I yell out?! I think I may have. I sit silently in the dark, calm my racing heart down, and listen. The voices continue off in the distance, still conversational; they don't change. No panic, no approaching footsteps.

I take off my boots and socks and quietly crawl through the door. Broken daylight filters in through dirty skylights, and here and there I can see more detail. Leaning against the wall stretching away in either direction away from me are the canvas covered backs of wooden frames holding paintings. And the ones next to me are big, at least three meters to a side.

I sit and listen; I can still hear the conversation, but I can't make anything out. It's coming from the far end of the warehouse—the front, near the outside lights.

I move slowly and cautiously, crawling low along the wall. I can make out the speakers as two German men. As I move closer, in between a gap in a stack of the framed canvases I can see into the warehouse.

In the center of the room is an artist's workstation—a large easel, chairs, and stools. Scattered on a large table next to the station are brushes, cans of turpentine, rags, light stands, scrapers, strainers, clean and used palettes, and hundreds of tubes of paint.

Beyond the artist's station is a wall with an open doorway leading into a living area at the front of the warehouse. Just inside I can see two men seated around a table talking, sipping coffee, and eating boiled eggs and pastries. The one I can see clearly is fat and balding; he gestures repeatedly as he speaks in loud tones. I can only just see the legs of the seated man he's talking to.

My stomach growls and cramps in anticipation at the sight of the food, and if I lean forward and put my ear to the gap I can begin to make out what's being said.

"We have to ask at least 1,000 marks, or we won't have enough money."

"And who is left that can afford that? Any civilian with that kind of cash still available has long since fled the country. They're waiting till after the war to return. And we can't go back to the military, *they'll confiscate him…AND us…worse, they'll kill us. You know we're liability."*

"All we need is three sales at 1,000 marks and we'll have enough to bribe a couple of convoy drivers and move everything northeast."

"And then what? Wait for the front to advance on us again? We need a way to get out. Leave the paintings and get us all out. That's much better. He's prolific; we'll just have to start over."

"I already told you, I'm not leaving all of this behind. We are sitting on a fortune here!"

"Yes, but he can always paint more!"

"But for how long? He deteriorates. His work will end one day. We need to hold on to every piece!"

"If the Allies overrun us here, which they will eventually, we'll be discovered, they're not going to just pass us over. And then…"

"Too bad we can't lock the warehouse up and just get out. Come back after and get them."

"Look, if they can't break in, they'll just blow the place up. They don't dare risk leaving an unexplored warehouse…"

"Alright, alright, enough. I'm getting a headache. Is he sleeping?"

"Yes, but I HAVE to stop giving him the morphine. I can hear fluid in his lungs again. And when he's on the morphine he doesn't cough it up. It's not good."

"Ahhh…You know what he's like when he doesn't sleep."

"Yes…But he needs to be clean for a few days."

"If you say so…I'm going back to Oberkirch this morning and speak to Marcel again. He told me last month he could still get his hands on trucks and men. If only he didn't want his money up front, if I could just talk him into waiting on payment…or think of something else for collateral. Maybe we should just sell the car. What else do you need?"

"I need salve and antibiotics, and I want to get some expectorant to get him coughing."

"Alright, come on, I'll drop you at the chemist on my way out. You can walk back. He'll stay under for several hours. You'll be back before he wakes."

The two men stand to leave. They continue talking as they walk out, and I hear a door outside shut behind them. They get in a car and drive away out the gate. I remain still for several more minutes, but hear nothing.

I finally stand and walk into the open warehouse. I'm opposite the artist's station. I stand in silence for several minutes listening, but I still hear nothing but the rain outside.

I move slowly out into the center of the warehouse. There's drab, broken light filtering in through glass skylights in the ceiling that have been partially painted over. All around me on all sides stretching back into the warehouse are paintings, row upon row of paintings. There must be at least two hundred of them that I can see: but my stomach croaks in protest again and reminds me of what's most important.

I step gingerly into the small apartment. The scent of cinnamon and coffee hang heavily in the air, and I'm suddenly woozy from the intensity of it. The plates are still on the table with the scraps of breakfast the two men have left. I grab the closest thing to me, a half-finished apple Danish, and greedily stuff it into my mouth, chew, and swallow.

The explosion of taste and smell that fills my senses knocks me to my knees, and I begin to sob. I chew and swallow as fast as I can. My stomach responds in loud gurgles and cramps, and I realize I'm going to be sick. It's too much all at once. I sit, then lay on the rug and try and breathe, and relax. I lay for several minutes until I feel solid enough to stand, and the wave of nausea hits me again and I crumple onto my back.

I lay there for the longest time, on my back staring at the ceiling, letting the molten pit of my stomach come to grips with food again, breathing, focusing, concentrating on the steel girders overhead, trying to staying awake, ready to crawl back to my little closet, but wanting desperately to eat more.

I eventually get back to my feet. The pantry is filled with bread and cheese, cans of fruit, condensed milk, honey, flour, sugar, bags of beans. In the small icebox I see weiswurst, hum, eggs, milk, butter. On the counter are bread, crackers, cans of soup, bottles of beer and wine. I take a couple of slices of bread, a hard-boiled egg, a few pieces of sliced lunchmeat from the refrigerator. I take a small box of matches, and I fill a glass with water, then I go back to my little opening in the warehouse, and crawl back to my closet.

I eat slowly and deliberately. I have to. While the food tastes wonderful, the open pit of my stomach fights and resists, recalling how to work on solid food again.

As I eat the last bite and swallow the last of my water, I can feel a headache starting, and I lay down to sleep, exhausted and relieved to at last have food and shelter.

I sleep for a while, I don't know how long, and when I wake and raise my head a dull throbbing greets me. My body feels odd and shaky, and my stomach is growling and cramping again, so I head back into the warehouse.

My leg aches from the wound, but my energy seems to be returning; standing is no longer a problem. I return to the kitchen, this time taking bread, more lunchmeat, and some cheese. I refill my glass with water.

As I slowly eat I walk around the apartment. The ceiling is low, much lower than the warehouse; this must be a converted front office. The front rooms are divided off with thin wood paneling, rugs on the floor, framed pictures on the walls. In a living area I find couches and chairs, a roll-top desk. On the opposite wall hangs a large swastika, the flag of the Reich. There's a hallway leading away to what I suppose are bedrooms.

I continue eating and walk from the apartment back out to the warehouse to the artist's area. A massive easel holds a large unfinished mural. From the back I can see the easel is mounted on counterweighted pairs of rollers that allow the painting to be moved up, down, left, or right. The artist's chair looks wobbly and awkward; elevated, with only one arm mounted on the right side of the chair, the seat and arm wrapped in white scraps of fabric and foam padding that are dirty and soiled, with smeared spots of old blood. The chair is on rollers, and it leans precariously.

The artist's worktable is also elevated, and covered with a dirty canvas tarp that holds stains and spills of all colors and varieties. Paints are strewn from one end to the other.

I turn to back to see the work on the easel and decide it's safe to snap on the portable light that's attached to the top.

What the light reveals is astonishing!

The painting is only two-thirds finished, a work in oil, but the mastery of the craft is obvious, even to me. I've only had the occasional visit to the museums in Frankfurt with Helga, but I've never seen anything like this.

The scenes in this painting seem to glow with richness and texture. The faces of the people appear to be alive with expression. Even the sky and clouds look eerily real. If I stare at them long enough I can almost imagine they are blowing slowly through the painting.

The perimeter of the canvas is ringed with scene after scene; a home and garden here, a schoolyard with children playing next to it. Below and to the left are teenagers lying in the grass under an apple tree, kissing, the girl's auburn hair gently tossed by the breeze, grackles rising off in flight in the distance. To the right a pair of horses race down a dirt roadway. Each scene flows seamlessly into the next. Brown grass in a field becomes the wall of a building in the scene beside it. A flowing brook here becomes a cobblestone street there.

In the center of the painting, larger than the surrounding scenes, stand a man and woman gazing and cooing at a small baby sleeping in the woman's arms. The woman's lips are lined and creased with age, the freckles that begin halfway down her neck are broken by the crisp white lace of her blouse. There are wisps of gray hair peeking out from beneath the man's fedora, and the faint shadows under his coat buttons make them appear to stand out in relief, away from the painting—I have to turn my head and glance sideways across the canvas to convince myself they aren't real.

The details are so accurate—the shadows that fill a dirty folded trouser hem, the dark cut of a scar across the man's forehead, even the stones and dirt leading up to a doorway. This isn't the imagined perfection of an ideal world that would *be so tempting to paint; these people look real, the lighting in the scenes is authentic, and I recognize a few of the settings from around Germany and Poland. It's almost as though this were some composite of photographs. I reach out and lightly feel the stiff texture of the dried brushstrokes.*

I stand astonished, taking this in, and then my focus moves to the far wall behind the easel. Stacked one upon the other is another, and another, and another; paintings just like this one, complete and finished.

The light that fills the warehouse is drab and broken, but even in the darkness and shadows, I can recognize enough detail. Some of the paintings are warm and bright, others dark and frightening.

In one, a German soldier is shot through the back in battle, his agony frozen in time as he falls forward to his death.

In the next, a tattooed man lies in a bunk in a jail cell in tears.

In another, a naked woman lies in bed caressing her lover as a man bursts through the bedroom door, knife in hand.

I gradually walk down the long open expanse of the warehouse and take in painting after painting, most large, some medium, and even a few small ones; all with the same incredible attention to detail, scenes, people, and composition.

One painting shows a mangled child lying in the road, apparently struck by a car, surrounded by adults screaming and crying.

Next to it, a young girl plays the harp, viewed from below the stage in the orchestra pit.

Another canvas portrays a young soldier standing in formation with his comrades, balancing buckets of water at arm's length, beads of sweat bursting from his forehead, intense concentration furrowing his brow.

I take this last painting in my hand and lean it forward; behind it is a group of kids dangling their feet off of a barn loft and jumping into the hay.

The painting behind that shows a barracks with floor-to-ceiling wooden bunks, crammed full with men, women, and children all dressed in gray, tattered rags.

In the one behind that, an SS guard stands at the edge of a pit, pointing a pistol at a bound prisoner's head below.

Behind that one, a man is making metal pots on a forging wheel in a factory.

And all of the paintings I see have the same compound scenery surrounding each one. Homes, and schools, gardens, cemeteries, churches. Weddings, Bar Mitzvahs, funerals. Children, the elderly, women and men. All flowing from one event to another. Scene after scene building story after story describing these lives.

And on, and on, and on, and on. I let the paintings I'm scanning fall back against the wall and do a slow turn around the warehouse. I don't know if I'm still woozy from lack of food or from the sheer magnitude of what I see. Painting after painting line the walls that surround me, all filled with the same subjects. Every one of them is a collage of people's lives, filled with their interactions. Some horrible, others beautiful. But I realize I don't see a single painting that's just a pastoral scene: a barn, a pasture, a row of crops, a thunderstorm over the mountains. All of what surrounds me is busy, and filled, and filled again with people and their relationships, in incredible, intense detail.

I have to sit down and close my eyes so that I don't fall.

Luka lowered the journal to stare at Erik, drugged and asleep on the cot. He tries to imagine what this man in front of him had just discovered.

Chapter 14

Back in the darkness of the closet I focus on my steps, retrace what I did, what I ate; did I cover my tracks? I replaced the half-eaten Danish on the plate with another from the kitchen. I dried and put back the glass I used. I looked for dirt, footprints that I might have left, turned off the easel lamp. Yes—I believe I've concealed my presence. I open up the stash of food I brought back with me for the night. Another Danish, crackers, a few slices of meat and cheese, olives, a tomato. Just an item here and there, each from a different jar, a single bag, hopefully not enough to be noticed.

But my mind keeps going back to the paintings, the exquisite scenery, the people so real you can reach out and touch them—so real they might turn their heads and smile at me—or worse, jeer back at me?

Off and on I doze through the night and into the next day in this cramped closet, sleeping propped up against the wall so that I don't snore. It's fitful sleep, but it's nice to be out of the wet and cold, and now I have the matches so I can see in the darkness.

Occasionally I dream of the dark gypsy girl. I see her smooth curved breast as I lay alongside her on top of a soft feather bed that we sink into. I decide it must be her bed, from her home, before the war. We spoon close against each other, she warms me as I wrap my arms around her and pull her close against me. I gently rub my hand back and forth along the small arch of her waist, lightly stroke the small hairs that I find there, and she moans softly in welcome response.

Periodically I'm woken by faint conversation, other times it's eerily quiet. I'm journaling a lot, writing about the events of the last few days, there's little else to do in here.

Once, I sneak out into the crawlway behind the paintings. I sit and listen but hear nothing, so I crawl back to the opening near the easel. Sit and listen again, but there's still no sound, except—I think maybe I can just faintly hear snoring? I finally decide it's safe for me to quickly get more food.

It's dusk, but enough dull light filters in through the skylights above me.

I go back into the kitchen, taking crackers and an apricot, and fill a glass with water. I turn back into the warehouse, to head to my hideout, but my attention is drawn to the artist's workstation. The work light has been left on, and there's a new mural with scenes having just been started, filling almost half of the canvas. Curious, I approach to see this new work.

My eyes go instantly to a scene in the center, from inside a small, sagging hunting cabin in the woods. And there I am, holding my gun against the brown gypsy woman's forehead, she holding the axe up in threat towards me!

I drop my glass in shock, shattering it across the floor, staggering backwards. I shake my head, trying to clear the image. Surely I've imagined this, I'm still dizzy from lack of energy and little food, that must be it!

But when I open my eyes again, the scene is still there, captured in amazing detail and vividness. I cannot believe what I'm seeing! The scene is exactly right, as if the painter was an observer there with us in the little hut to witness it—me crouching in the doorway, Luger pointed at her head, she trying to counter my threat, wielding the heavy axe.

How is this possible?!

I pry my eyes away to the top of the canvas to find more scenes. They all have in common a beautiful young, dark-skinned girl. In this one she's very young, a child, skipping along a stone path holding an adult's hand, eating an apple; in the next playing with several other children in a mud puddle along a cart path at a fair, in this one smiling and dancing with an older woman, dressed in a belly dancer's outfit at a party; in the next wrapped up close in a thick horse blanket in the loft of a barn, holding the hand of a teenage boy, a lost look in her eyes.

And then one scene takes my breath away—there she is, maybe sixteen years old, dressed in a leotard, posed on one leg in front of the railing and mirror of a dance studio. In the reflection of the mirror an older woman is using a long wooden rod to tap out a metronome beat against the barre.

I can't take my eyes off of her; it's definitely my gypsy girl. Her features are younger, but breaking through the smooth cut of her high cheeks, the thin sinew of her arms, the concentration etched on her face, I can see the woman I met in the cabin. Somehow she is here, captured before our encounter.

Below the dance scene is another of her with maybe twenty other people being loaded onto trucks by German soldiers, machine guns pointed, the group moving in fear, in tears. In the next I see her and several other young girls mopping a concrete floor, eyes down, hair pulled back under scarves, concentrating hard on the job at hand, SS soldiers standing at attention against a far wall.

My heart is now pounding away in my chest, in fear for her.

Then in the next scene, she is naked, arms desperately trying to cover her pubis and chest, standing before an SS officer. The smooth small curve of breast that she's not completely able to hide is unmistakable. The officer smirking as he reaches out...

"NOOOO!" I yell, in disbelief. I stagger, slipping on the water I spilled, and grab the easel as I fall, pulling it and the painting down on top of me.

I stand, hurry to the kitchen, and yank open drawers. I'm reacting, not even sure what I'm looking for. How can this possibly be, who painted this? Who else has seen this?

And then I spy what I'm searching for: a small, sharp paring knife.

I race back into the warehouse, to the painting lying face-up on the floor, and stab into the center of the scene with my gypsy girl, embarrassed and naked, about to be violated. I rip sideways and tear across the canvas, cutting slashes randomly through the fabric. I cut through the scene of me holding the gun to her head, I cut through her holding the teenage boy in the loft.

And then I fall back to the floor, sobbing, in shock. "How is this happening?" I repeat over and over to myself.

When I look back at the canvas, the torn shards of fabric make the scenes impossible to recognize now, and I begin to calm. I look down and recognize the shattered glass and water that now litter the floor and I remember yelling. I wonder why I haven't been confronted yet? The men must be away. I got lucky for once. Bit by bit, I return to my senses.

I find a dish towel in the kitchen to soak up the water, then sweep the broken glass and crackers I spilled into the center, and stuff the entire wet mess into my pants pocket. I reset the easel and try to reassemble the workstation the way I remember it. I return to the torn canvas, and just as I go to lift it from the floor, I hear the crunch of gravel, and see headlights sweep across the tiny cracks of the front door of the warehouse.

I run to the closest stack of paintings against the wall, pull them back, and place the ruined canvas last, leaning the stack back against the wall. I can hear muffled conversation and the shuffle of shoes on gravel as I duck behind the stack.

Before I go back to my closet, I sit and listen to the level and tone of the conversation, heart pounding, trying to detect whether I've announced myself with all my destruction. Please, just maybe, the missing canvas won't be noticed until morning, and by then I will be gone.

I lay still, listening, but the voices sound normal, the conversation regular and even, nothing unusual.

As I start to crawl back to my closet and pack my things to leave, my face brushes the torn fabric of the painting I've just destroyed, and I stop. I sit up, crouched behind it, back against the wall, and try to peer through the darkness to figure out what scene I'm looking at, but I can't identify it. I can just barely make out dark and light areas, no *detail. Concentrating as hard as I can does no good. There's not enough light here.*

Then I remember—the knife is still in my pocket, and what I do next is instinctual. I take the knife and slowly cut away the flap of canvas, to take back to the closet with me.

Safely back in my little room I close the door, find the box of matches, light one, and gasp! It's the scene of my gypsy girl, dancing in her leotard in the studio.

Here, alone, over the initial shock, I can examine the scene more carefully. The detail and color are even more beautiful than at first site. Her legs are covered thigh to feet in white stockings, ending in faded pink toe shoes. She is standing high on the toes of her left foot, her right foot pulled up and resting gracefully at a forty-five degree angle against her inner left thigh. Right arm lightly holding the bar, the left spread gracefully and sweeping behind, head bowed in a slight, confident smile.

The details are reassuring to me. The too-long wisp of hair that's escaped and fallen from her bun, and now dangles along her ear. I remember seeing that in the cabin! Her hand cupped along the wooden rail, the same way she grabbed the can of peaches from me.

In the dancing light of the match, her expression appears to change. Wait, now she's looking at me! No, that can't be...it's my imagination.

"My little brown gypsy," I whisper, and I smile.

Instead of packing to leave, I stare at my painting, burning match after match, until I fall asleep; and for the first time in quite a long while I sleep soundly through the night.

When I wake the next morning I crack the door and let in the drab light from the warehouse. I reach out to touch my new work of art, but I can't find it. I left it propped up behind a run of wires on the wall in front of me, and it's not there!

In a panic I feel around the floor, and instead find the box of matches. I quickly take one out to light it, and break it off in the attempt. "Damn it!" I protest out loud, not caring who hears me. I push the door open as wide as it will go to let more light in, and I just spy my scrap of painting in the corner.

It must have slipped down the wall during the night. My little brown gypsy is still here...such a relief. My small treasure is safe. I decide right then to hide her in a place where I alone can always find her. I take the knife and cut a slit into my checkered jacket, in the inner lining of the left side, just under the armpit, and I slip my little brown gypsy inside, where I know she is safe.

Luka dropped the journal and sat bolt upright. In the corner of the basement, in a pile, were Erik's clothes, including the checkered wool hunting jacket. Luka went over, picked up the jacket, and reached inside, feeling the lining under the left arm until his finger slipped inside an opening—a long slit between the inner and outer linings. Slowly and carefully feeling inside, lower and lower, his finger finally brushed against a scrap of something. He carefully pulled it out and walked over to the reading lamp.

Now it was Luka's turn to gasp. In his hand was the scrap of painting, the gypsy dancer, and it was everything Erik had described, and more.

Chapter 15

Luka sat, turning the portion of painting over and over in his hands, waiting for Erik to awaken. He had reached the end of the journal; everything after was empty pages, leaving unanswered questions. So Luka skipped the noon shot of morphine, and sat patiently waiting for Erik to wake. He had all the background he could obtain. It was time to get his answers directly from the source.

Luka's primary area of art expertise was sculpture, but he had studied classical and romantic painting through five years of a college art major. He was considered by both the establishment and the underground to be a quick and accurate judge of quality. And the small scrap of work he held in his hands was remarkable. The fine edge of detail that lined the subjects, the smooth brushwork, the choice of color, the subtle shadows and nuances of the room, the exquisite expression of both people; even the sparse spread of oils, and the canvas itself all spoke of a meticulous attention to quality.

But even more mysterious than the sum of the details was the mesmerizing allure of the overall work itself. The girl's face radiated dark beauty, tranquility, and concentration while the teacher's face spoke of sternness and detachment, but also a sad longing.

The painting this scrap had been cut from was very modern, almost as if it had been somehow pulled from a photograph. Luka could discern no trained technique or copied style. The work was unique, and mesmerizing.

He lowered the scrap of painting to find Erik looking around, blinking slowly. His expression was one of confusion, unfamiliarity. His gaze met Luka's, as he blinked slowly and mouthed words with no sound.

"What?" Luka asked.

WATER, Erik mouthed again more slowly.

"Oh...sorry." Luka stammered in response. "Of course, here." Luka refilled a glass he had already been using from his canteen.

Erik grabbed it greedily with both hands and gulped the water. He choked and sputtered, but didn't stop until he had finished the glass, then thrust it forward. He winced in pain as he did so, nearly dropping the glass.

"More?" Luka inquired?

Erik nodded in response.

Luka spoke while he refilled the glass. "You dislocated your arm when you fell...in the alley...do you remember?"

Erik drank, continuing to stare at Luka, then he paused to speak in raspy tones, "Yes...I think so. You're..." he paused trying to think, "the art dealer?"

"That's right."

"The spy," Erik added, and handed the glass back for a third refill.

Luka didn't answer as he filled and handed the glass across.

Erik paused and blinked, gazing around the basement.

"You're in Trier. In an abandoned boardinghouse. Being cared for."

Luka noticed that Erik's gaze was fixed on the journal sitting on the bedside table.

"You've been reading my journal?" Erik asked.

"Yes," Luka answered directly and without hesitation. He was studying the reactions of the man before him while he fingered the scrap of painting in his pocket.

"Well...I see." And then a pause, "I understand....considering..."

Suddenly a look of panic crossed Erik's face, "Uh...would you bring me my jacket, the checked wool coat?" Erik pointed frantically to the pile of clothes in the corner and winced again as he tried to push himself up in the bed.

"You're looking for this..." Luka produced the painting scrap from his pocket and held it out to Erik.

"Yes!" Erik snatched the scrap out of Luka's hand and began stroking the surface of it gently, reassuringly. A smile crossed his face, and his demeanor relaxed.

Luka didn't speak directly, observing the man. The silence passed between them for a long time until Erik finally broke it with a whisper, "My little brown gypsy."

Luka responded, "Look, I know your story now..."

Erik broke out in a hoarse laugh, still gazing at the scrap of painting. "You only know part of my story." Now he was looking at Luka again. "What's in the journal, it's only the beginning...of something unbelievable."

Luka held his gaze, expecting Erik to break into his alleyway rantings. But Erik just held Luka's stare.

"Alright," Luka answered as he sat down across from Erik. "But why me? Why did you come here looking for me?"

"Because you can get it all out. The paintings...those incredible..." Erik's face had changed, he was distressed again, Luka could see the beginnings of the intensity he had observed back in the square.

Luka just shook his head slowly in doubt.

"I know, I know," Erik said, shaking his own head in reply. He looked away and laughed in response. "Believe me, I know it doesn't make sense. Let me finish the story for you."

"I wasn't able to get out of the utility closet in time. They came and dragged me out early in the morning. They took me and locked me away in a bedroom in the apartment in the front of the warehouse. The two men that took me, I recognized one, Colonel Alfred Wirths, very high up in the Reich, well known. I've seen pictures of him. The colonel at one time was commandant at one of the prisoner-of-war camps in Poland. The other man I didn't know, but the colonel kept calling him 'Doctor.' They said they knew my history, where I had been, and that I was a deserter. The colonel said I should be handed over to the SS. I didn't know how at the time, but they knew everything about me."

"Well, I just fell apart. Spent the day crying mostly, and sleeping some, probably from exhaustion. I suppose I had always expected to be caught. I guess I was relieved in a way."

"But then in the evening, the doctor brought me dinner and tended to my leg. He said they had something very important to show me. But not now, I needed to have patience."

"I suspected they would still just turn me in. Then later in the evening the doctor came back again to get me. They took me out in the center of the warehouse, and there on the easel in the middle at the workstation...was something unbelievable. It was my painting, my life story, started, just like my gypsy girl's painting. Just like I had seen in the other paintings surrounding the warehouse."

He turned and nodded to Luka knowingly. To Luka, it looked like Erik had drifted away, lost in some hypnotizing daydream. Erik stared off toward the far wall and appeared to be gazing intently beyond, summoning some remarkable vision.

"The painting started in the upper left corner, with me as a young boy growing up in Frankfurt. It showed me at school, then playing soccer, then the death of my father when I was six, my sister Helga and me playing in the chalk caves down at the river when I was nine; it was remarkable, a retelling of my life. Then it showed when I joined the Youth Corps at school and started training for the army, the camp at Stadt, my first battle in the north of France when I was so terrified. Then being pushed back into the Rhein Valley, the mortar that exploded in our foxhole and killed Heisse, all in remarkable detail. Each scene flowed from one to another, like a river winding around and through the canvas."

"And then it showed my desertion, me crawling out of the foxhole, walking through the river valley by night, my two nights at the cabin."

"But then," Erik paused to look directly at Luka. "It showed me in the warehouse, with all of the paintings, hiding in the little utility closet, stealing food, and staring at the easel."

Erik's eyes were wild, while he watched Luka for a response.

"Don't you get it? They had a painting of me...my life's story. From my birth, all the way up to finding the warehouse."

Luka sat stoically, eyes narrowed in disbelief.

"I know, I know...I don't blame you. But you didn't see this, I did. I'm not crazy. I saw it with my own eyes. That's how they found me...it was in the painting...it showed them my hiding place in the closet."

Luka finally responded, "You must have been drugged from the food they brought you. Or you were still delirious from hunger."

Erik was nodding his head. "I told myself the same thing, this can't be real. But I wasn't drugged the first two nights I hid in there. I asked the doctor how they had this, how could this be possible? But he wouldn't answer me. All he would say is, 'it's a miracle, isn't it,' and grinned back at me."

Luka carefully observed Erik.

"I'll tell you, I was in shock. I couldn't sleep."

"The next morning they brought me breakfast, and the doctor's demeanor had changed, he was much nicer to me. He dressed my leg wound, applied ointment, and gave me some pills for the pain. He told me something had changed, and I might be able to help us all out now."

"He took me back out into the warehouse, and there was an addition to my painting! Get ready for this...it was you and me in the square in Trier. It was me walking across the square calling out to you, and you at the café, standing in shock, looking back at me, the woman baker standing in the doorway, dropping the plate. All the detail was exactly right, your black coat draped over a chair next to your table."

Erik paused. All Luka could do was stare back at Erik in disbelief.

"Now do you see why I was so delirious that day in the square? Do you understand now?...somehow they were showing me my future, before it had even happened!"

Erik paused, then looked away and shook his head.

"Fantastic, I know." Then Erik's dreamy demeanor bled away, and he glared. "But then their tone turned ugly. The colonel started questioning me. 'Where is this place,' pointing at the square in the painting, and who were you, and the woman behind you? I didn't know, of course; I had never seen any of it, and I didn't have a clue who you were. But he persisted, asking me over and over, like they didn't believe me. The colonel grew furious. He started yelling and threatening me. He said that he would turn me over to the SS.

But I just didn't know, I couldn't even think of an answer to make up for them!"

"So he threw me back in the apartment, locked me in. In the evening they came and brought me dinner, and soon after I began to feel sick. I fell asleep feeling really strange, and the room was spinning wildly."

"When I woke up I was in a moving car, my head was covered, and my hands were bound. I didn't say anything for a long time, pretended to be asleep, but then I could hear the colonel's voice; he started to talk, but the doctor hushed him immediately—he said I was awake. The colonel asked if he was sure, and the doctor answered, 'yes, the drug has been timed, don't say anything else.'"

"I didn't make a sound, or any movement. Now I was sure I was going to be shot. I was terrified, and I lay as still as I could. We drove for some time, but finally we came to a stop, and the doctor grabbed me by the arm and pulled me out of the car. He cut the rope binding my hands and pulled the hood off of my head. We were on an empty road, leading up to a village, just before dawn. The colonel walked over and tossed my belongings at my feet.

"Then the doctor said, 'You're where you need to be; the town square in the painting is just up the hill in that village, Trier. In the square you will find the art dealer, Luka Meiter. He's an Allied spy, but he can help us, all of us, he can help you too. Go and convince him to come, to help us move all of the paintings to safety, we know he has the resources at his disposal to pull it off. If you do this, we'll give you your life's painting for free, the one you've already seen. It will be yours to do with as you will, and you'll be free to go. Oh…and it will be finished, the rest of your life, right up to your death, everything you could possibly want to know about your future. That's worth it, yes?' and then he laughed. 'Bring Luka the spy, convince him to come and help us, and the painting is yours. That's the price of the muse.' Then he turned, laughing, heading back to the car to leave.

'Wait!' I shouted after him. 'I don't even know where you're located.'

The doctor turned back to me. 'Haslach,' he answered, 'The warehouse is just South of Haslach. We'll be there, waiting.'

Luka laughed and stood, "You were drugged. I mean not just in the car, the whole time, you were drugged. Listen to yourself; this couldn't have happened. It's simply not possible."

But Erik didn't flinch or look away. A slow grin crept across his mouth. "They told me you would say that, so they gave me something else, a gift for you. Look in the slit in my coat jacket."

"I already looked there," Luka snapped back. "I found the gypsy painting, remember?"

"Look again, it should still be there," Erik replied.

Luka stared back at Erik, but he didn't look irrational, he looked utterly serious. Luka turned, went back to the pile of clothes, and picked up the coat. While he kept his eyes on Erik he felt again along the jacket lining. He found the precision slit under the arm, and felt inside again, running his finger back and forth.

"There's nothing in here," Luka said angrily.

"Dig deeper, it might have slipped farther down."

Luka picked up the coat with both hands and pressed the bottom of the jacket against his searching finger. And then he brushed something, another piece of canvas. Slowly and gingerly he eased the cloth to the slit and out of the jacket. While he kept his eyes on Erik he walked back to the lamp.

In his hands was another scrap of painting, this time torn away from the original, leaving ragged edges. It was a scene of the square in Trier, Erik hobbling away from the clock tower toward the café, Luka standing, watching Erik's progress in alarm, reaching for his black overcoat draped across the chair, behind him Claudia with her hand to her mouth, dropping the plate; the moment perfectly, magically, and beautifully frozen in time.

Chapter 16

Luka squatted low on the rise beside the church and peered through the dusk focused on the old tilted hay barn. The signal plank was gone, no longer leaning against the hinge. He hadn't seen the other sign he was looking for yet, but he was certain Jack must be in the barn waiting for him. The shortwave broadcast from that morning had transmitted the urgency of their meeting tonight:

NO WAITING <STOP> FOUND OTHER
SOURCE <STOP> TONIGHT OR NOT
AT ALL – NO DELAYS <STOP>

Luka reached into his pocket and pulled out his new scrap of painting. He had lost count of how many times he had looked at the frozen moment in the square—as if looking at it again might convince him that it was real—and yet there it was, somehow a moment of his life vividly captured before it had even happened. Every detail was laid out flawlessly: Luka's stunned look, Erik hobbling across the square, Claudia dropping the plate, mouth agape. Even the minor details were striking:

the worn cobblestones of the square, the thin black table and chair legs at the café, the worn paint chipping off the frame of the café doorway. He touched the precious piece of canvas, trying in vain to have it make sense.

He slipped the prize back in his pocket, watched the barn with his binoculars again, and finally saw the second telltale sign of Jack's, the bright red dot of a cigar tip as it was being drawn on; he was there inside, waiting. Luka stood and began the long walk down the road to the abandoned farm. He knew Jack would be mad at Luka's departure from schedule and then missing the cover trip to Albstadt.

For the hundredth time that day Luka tried to think of some new piece of information that could be added to the facts that would somehow convince Jack to let him go find the warehouse and the paintings, some way to weave it into his next mission. As he walked, he fingered the scrap of canvas in his pocket. He felt sure he could uncover what Erik hadn't been able to, the mystery behind this snapshot of their lives. But there was something else nagging at him, something else that he knew he should answer before he entered the barn. He paused at the doorway trying to identify the question, and then went inside.

Luka entered the barn to find Jack methodically pacing back and forth between the barn doors and a far window. He was puffing wildly on his cigar, dirty blue smoke filled the space. Now Jack was pacing back toward Luka, staring him directly in the eyes. He kept coming until stopping a few feet short of Luka's face.

"Well?" Jack's baritone voice resonated, filling the hollow shell of the barn. Luka jumped at the volume of it. Jack was never this loud outside, in the open, exposed. Before Luka could answer, Jack spun on his heels and walked back to the far window.

"Jack..." Luka started, but didn't know where to go next. He didn't dare offer an apology right away, he knew better. He had seen Jack verbally rip apart young recruits at moments similar to this one.

"Five days," Jack rumbled low into the darkness of the barn. "You were two days overdue to the courier from your last mission, and you were supposed to be in Albstadt three days ago."

Now Jack was walking back toward him. "Five days!" He held up the fingers of his spread hand in emphasis.

"I know," Luka answered. "I was assaulted in Trier, five days ago, by..."

"The deserter?" Jack interrupted.

Luka stopped, stunned, staring at Jack's back as he paced away again.

"Yes," Luka managed to state, but the answer came out sounding more like a question.

"Your doctor has a big mouth," Jack answered. "He's afraid he's going to get caught should the SS come looking, so he's already been talking; the word is out. He's a good little Nazi. You're just incredibly lucky the front has gotten so close to Trier—the SS are too busy with bigger problems." Jack was staring at him, only a few feet away again, "But they haven't forgotten, they'll definitely be coming for your deserter shortly."

A chill ran up Luka's back. Now he knew why Jack was so furious. He had screwed up big, and until now he hadn't realized just how big, spending all of his time trying to unravel the mysteries of Erik.

Jack continued his pacing in silence, letting Luka stew in his own thoughts.

Luka's mind was racing now, and it didn't help being in here, Jack pacing, in the ruins of the old barn, full of cigar smoke. The exposed windows and crooked ceiling seemed to be staring back at him, accusing him, waiting for an answer too, focusing Jack's anger, like a mad gallery funhouse. The structure seemed animated, ready to exact Jack's punishment upon him.

In his fascination with the encounter in the square and Erik's journal, he had forgotten to pay attention. Jack's first rule: pay attention—read your surroundings. Always, always, pay attention. And the second rule? Where are your weak points? The doctor...of course, how stupid and arrogant of Luka. He pinched his eyes closed and lowered his head in disgust. He had royally screwed up.

Luka looked at Jack, who was still pacing, watching him think, waiting patiently for more. It was Luka's turn to explain.

"The deserter…He knew things about me, Jack. He knew that I'm a spy, that I'm not really German. He was blurting it out loud, in the square!"

Jack stopped inches away from his face again. "Then why didn't you kill him?" he asked matter-of-factly.

That was the simplest answer to the situation in the square that day. It's what Jack would have done. It's what he'd been trained to do.

"What he knew, Jack, it was strange. He wasn't coming after me or accusing me. He wanted my help. He was yelling my name out in the alley, in front of witnesses, almost like he was begging me to help him. I couldn't just kill him there. I needed some time to get more information out of him. To find out how he knew what he knew. A day at the most…"

"You're not an interrogator, you're an observer. Your job is information gathering." Jack continued his pacing. "You know that."

"I know, Jack…I know. But then he collapsed in my arms in the alley, and witnesses were there before I could do anything."

Jack was in front of him again. "Five days," he said in a low growl. "You had plenty of time to kill him."

Luka slumped, out of excuses.

After a long pause Jack finally responded. "Good God! Four years in the field, and you never messed up once, you've been one of the best kids I've ever trained. You have always been like clockwork, and you've always produced good usable intelligence. When they gave you to me I said an art dealer cover was the most absurd thing I've ever heard of, but you pulled it off. I was impressed."

"And then you go and pull this little stunt, go completely off schedule, unplug from the grid for five whole days. I was afraid that you might have exposed the whole southern operation."

"Jack...you're right. I get what you..."

"Well I hope you do, because I'm pulling you out," Jack answered and turned to walk away again.

"What?" Luka stammered. "Because of this?"

Jack stopped suddenly and turned slowly to face him again. "Luka, people start dying when someone screws up like this." He paused to let the point sink home, then turned and continued his pacing. "Let's just leave it at...your little stunt has accelerated existing plans. You messed up, but no harm— no foul. You weren't uncovered, you're alive, you weren't captured. No one else has been exposed yet. As far as we know, the SS has only realized that your friend is a deserter, and they still believe you're a german smuggler."

Jack turned back toward the window. "Is the deserter still alive?"

"Yes." Luka stared at the floor, trying to clear his head, to think.

"Then let's salvage this situation right now. The front is almost on your doorstep. I would have had to pull you out in a few weeks anyway. I was going to move you north, toward Berlin, keep you working, but that can't happen now."

Luka was walking in circles now, trying to think. "No...no" was all he could manage to get out. He stopped to think of what he could say next, how to change this.

"Jack...look. There's one more thing I have to do before you pull me out." Luka fumbled.

Jack had stopped pacing and was staring straight at him, waiting for Luka to continue.

"You remember the reports we had last winter, that the Nazis had stolen massive art collections from the national museums in France, Norway, and Holland, and moved them back across the border into Germany?"

Jack didn't move.

"Erik...the deserter. He stumbled across one of those stashes, I'm sure of it. Hundreds of paintings. He was hiding there, in an abandoned warehouse, after he deserted."

Luka waited for a response, but none came.

"He had evidence, Jack, accurate descriptions. I believe his story. The timeline makes sense. And he brought back scraps, pieces of canvas. I've examined them, I think it's real."

"Where are these scraps?" Jack snapped. "Did you bring them with you?"

Luka momentarily considered revealing the prized bit of painting he now carried, but he didn't dare; it would definitely confuse the argument, or worse, make Jack suspicious. Erik and Luka in the same painting, it was all too strange to try to explain on top of everything else.

"They're back at the boardinghouse, with Erik," Luka finally replied.

"And where is this warehouse?" Jack followed.

Luka shook his head, still unsure of how much he needed to divulge to convince Jack. "I'm not exactly sure. It was while he was deserting, and he was lost for a time, walking for days. I've retraced the route I think he most likely took from his journal, it's most likely near Haslach. But I'm not completely certain."

"Haslach?" Jack sneered. "Haslach is about to fall, a week at the most from being overrun."

Luka stared at his feet, trying to think. "Shit" was all he could manage.

"How were you planning to find this warehouse?" Jack asked.

Luka closed his eyes hard at the next answer, but there was no point in lying about it, he was already in over his head anyway. "I was going to take Erik with me." The words tumbled out.

Jack scoffed. "Really? You were going to take a Nazi deserter out in the field, possibly a spy sent to infiltrate your operation, manage to squeeze in between an active front, and recover a cache of stolen art?" The plan sounded thoroughly absurd upon Jack's retelling. "Did you also want me to send a parade of moving trucks in with you?"

Luka didn't bother to answer.

"You'll be sure to shoot me up a flare when you find it, ok?" he added, snickering.

"Forget it, kid, it's too late. The art's always been secondary, you know that." Jack turned to look, but Luka was shaking his bowed head, not listening.

"You know what, kid?" Jack sneered. His tone had changed from lecturing to something lower and brooding. "When I'm in the field, managing my crews, sometimes I think the worst, I can't help it. It's my problem, mind you, I agonize over the bad possibilities, endlessly. What do I do if this or that has happened? If I don't stop, I can't sleep at night." Jack paused, now walking slowly toward Luka. And a few days ago it crossed my mind, maybe my kid in Trier has turned."

Luka looked up, stunned, to meet Jack's stare.

"I wondered how long you've been playing me. Maybe you've been running both sides for some time now."

"No," Luka whispered.

"Yeah?" Jack paused "You sure? Because right now you look and sound half-crazy with this talk of an abandoned warehouse full of art, and sneaking off into an active war zone to find it with a Nazi deserter. Not the shrewd intel gatherer I've come to know."

Luka held Jack's gaze, frozen, unable to respond.

"The art...don't...matter." Jack spoke slowly, deliberately. Waiting for a sign of recognition in response, Luka nodded slowly.

"Yeah?" Jack repeated. Luka continued nodding, not looking up.

"Alright," Jack finally continued. "Then here's exactly what's happening next. You're going back to your apartment. You're going to gather your orders, your code book, mission dockets, notes, whatever paperwork you have hidden, all of it, anything incriminating, the whole package. You're listening, RIGHT?" Jack shouted at him.

"Yes," Luka answered flatly.

"Then you're going to...LOOK AT ME!" Jack snapped.

Luka looked up at him suddenly.

Jack paused to let the next sentence sink in. "You're going to kill the deserter... quietly...cleanly. You leave the body, then you come back here and wait for pickup inside the bunker. Understood?"

"Yes," Luka whispered.

"No questions, right? You're being pulled out. This isn't a discussion, it's an order. I'm having your courier meet you here at daybreak with transport. And that's the end of it. You shuttle back across the lines into France and you start debriefing. Forget the warehouse, forget the art, forget the deserter, they're not worth it. You wind up back home, and then you'll thank your lucky stars in a month that I was here, and that you listened right now."

Jack paused, he seemed to be waiting for a reaction. "You clear?"

"Yes," Luka answered.

Jack stared at Luka as if there might be more to say, then tossed the stub of his cigar to the ground, crushing it into the dirt. "Good," he added, then strode past Luka out into the night.

Part II – The Journey

Chapter 17

A warm afternoon hugged the little suburb of Sharcross, Minnesota, with just the occasional high scud of a lone cumulus cloud to break the sun, a confirmation that the short, wet spring was drawing to a close, and the promise of a hot, sunny summer lay just around the corner. Luka alternated between watching the children and chimney swifts chasing june bugs, and his father carefully painting the window trellis a ruddy brown in typical silent, deep concentration. Luka had been sitting next to his father for the past thirty minutes, searching for how to begin the conversation that he wanted desperately to have over. Unable to find a good way to start, he stumbled in.

"Dad?"

"Hmmm."

"I talked to Professor Pennington again today." Luka paused to let the opening start pulling its gravity, but he got no reaction.

"He still wants me to come, early...in mid-July, maybe even earlier. He says I can work summer crew on campus, and he'll help me locate a grant. But that I need to be there, making my own pieces to show. Showing my work is important for me to have any chance at a grant. He knows a group of gallery owners in New York that have sponsored students in the past. He'll put in a good word for me."

"I thought we already decided this," his father mumbled into the trellis.

Luka didn't answer. The sinking feeling was already starting in the pit of his stomach.

"What are you going to do for money?"

"I can work on a summer crew for room and board. I called and checked. They have openings."

His father stood and let go a deep sigh, not taking his eyes from his work. "A sculptor?" the words landed flat between the two of them, dripping of judgment and disdain.

Luka could feel the blood flushing his face now. "Yes," he managed. "Why not? Pennington likes my work. He says I show promise. He knows money is tight, but he really thinks he can find me something when I get there. I know you think it's risky..." Luka trailed off.

"You know why not. Because it's not a career is why not. Because you should stop playing with your clay and paints, and find a real job that earns real money. That's why not."

There was a familiar awkward silence between the older and younger man, neither looking at the other.

"I want to go, Dad, I want to do this..."

After a long silence, he added, "It's my life" in anger.

Luka's father turned and marched off of the porch. "Biggest mistake you'll ever make" his father added over his shoulder.

Luka slumped low in the front seat of the roadster, below the top of the seat back, but high enough to clearly keep watch on the back door of the boardinghouse. By parking across the street the evening before, he could discretely walk the alleys back to his apartment, pack, be back here to finish with Erik, and then make a quick escape by daybreak.

The familiar pit at the bottom of his stomach had returned. He just wasn't sure which conversation had brought it on this time; the memory of the one not so long ago with his father on that Minnesota porch, or the recent one with Jack ordering him to pack up and kill the deserter.

Flashes of light on the southern horizon interrupted his thoughts, and the deep rumble of artillery shell bursts announced that the war was moving closer to Trier.

Most of the crust of the past four years of his life had been left where it stood in his apartment, but the deep layers, the incriminating things—the documents, notes, maps, recordings, any item that could point back to his role as a spy— had all been stuffed neatly into the fat leather storage pouch that now lay tucked beneath the well of the passenger seat.

He felt utterly vulnerable. Any German patrolman that might wander along now, and just happen to take an interest, could piece together the whole of his cover, and what he was really engaged in, with just a few hours reading. It was all right there, packaged neatly for convenience. Luka had always been careful to keep his documents elaborately hidden and separate, so that if one were found, it wouldn't entirely implicate him on its own. There was some reassurance in the fact that it would take work to piece his real life together; but now, here it all was, packaged up in one nice bundle.

The weight of the Luger in his lap brought him back to the conversation in the barn from the evening before. Jack was right, of course; the logical thing to do was to end this. The war was closing in, and the area would grow highly dangerous very quickly. Jack had hinted before that Luka might get moved north to continue surveillance; but now he had screwed up, risked getting caught.

In four years of spying he had built an impressive resumé of surveillance. He could finally relax in France and debrief for the next few months; wait for the end of the war, stop looking over his shoulder every day. There would be a lot of work left to do—maybe he could even stay in France and coordinate the rest of the spies as they came in from the field as the war drew to a close. At one point Jack had talked to him about training and managing his own crew. He still might be able to push for that. Staying close to the action appealed to him.

Luka sighed and pressed his back into the seat to stretch, one hand on the Luger in his lap, the other fingering the scrap of painting in his pocket. Soon his life in Trier would be at an end. Seeing it now in retrospect, it was shocking to him just how far his life had turned to get here.

And then his daydreaming abruptly stopped. He stiffened as a constable walked into the light of the corner street lamp across from the alley entrance. The man stopped, to look down, fumbling with something in his hands. He had heard of SS officers dressing as constables and guards, and the man he watched now wasn't familiar to him. Luka snapped off the gun's safety and caressed the rough knurling of the trigger with his left index finger, while his right hand drifted back to the scrap of painting, like a reflex. Even in the shadows, hidden from the light, its pull on him was seductive.

He watched carefully as the constable fumbled with whatever was in his grasp, then reached both hands up to his mouth and pulled a pouch drawstring closed with his teeth; he was rolling a cigarette. Luka relaxed as the man lit it, took a long draw, and then blew a thick blue stream of smoke into the night air. The constable strode slowly out from under the lamp, past the corner shop, and back into the dark of night. Luka stuffed the pistol into the rear of his pants. It would be light in a few hours; it was time to move.

Quietly, cautiously, Luka cleared first the main floor, then the top floor of the old boardinghouse. His senses in high gear due to Jack's warning, he took his time, listening, observant, making sure no one was hiding in the shadows.

After he was satisfied, he moved down the old stairway into the basement, stopping to listen as he went, pistol drawn, ready for whatever might be coming. Pausing on the bottom landing, he could just hear Erik's quiet snoring. That's when it came to him, the answer to the unspoken question that had nagged at him back at the barn. He would find a way to go see the paintings, he was sure of it.

In the basement now, Luka moved slowly around to the head of the cot and bent down to grab the extra pillow stored there. Erik woke with a start; seeing the gun in Luka's one hand, the pillow coming rapidly toward his face with the other, and with terror in his eyes, he began to struggle.

"Shhh, shhhh. It's alright," Luka whispered. "It's alright, quiet!"

Luka loosened the pillow enough for Erik to stop struggling. "You've been discovered. I just needed to make sure you were quiet before I woke you up. That's all. The SS could be nearby, waiting."

Erik drew loud raspy breaths in and out through his nose, trying to calm down. Luka still held the pillow gently to his mouth. They stayed that way for some time, Luka listening, Erik panting, trying to regain some composure, staring back at Luka, not trusting him.

"We're leaving, now. You and I, together."

Erik nodded slowly in silent agreement. Luka finally dropped the pillow to the floor.

"The doctor. He talked. Told them you were a deserter. We're both in serious danger here. Let's go. Quietly."

Getting Erik dressed and up the stairway took longer than Luka had expected. Five days of bed rest, sore shoulder, and wounded leg combined to make him gangly and awkward. By the time they had reached the car, the first orange yawnings of dawn were peaking up the eastern horizon.

Luka started the roadster and eased it down the cobblestone alley, leaving the lights off. It was still too early to clear curfew, but they were safer moving than sitting in the car and waiting for sunrise. At each street crossing he paused to look carefully but saw no one. Another cross street and they arrived at the main road out of town. They turned onto it, heading north, away from the barn and away from his scheduled rendezvous, toward Haslach instead.

Chapter 18

The sweat had long-since soaked through his bandana and T-shirt, and it was now dripping onto anything he bent over to carry in; boxes, desks—all came away stained with large round drops of his effort. It was early June, in upstate New York, but the campus air conditioners had all been turned off to save money. It was already a sauna in the long physics lab, even though it was just past ten in the morning and all the windows were wide open. But Luka was happy.

The work was tedious and paid next to nothing. But for the first time in his life he felt untethered, free to move in whatever direction suited him best. His newfound freedom brought relief, a dizzying lightheadedness of possibility; but it also came with an unexpected hollowness, something incomplete that rang of unspoken hopes.

He had decided to move in early June, right after high-school graduation. Forego the road trip to Chicago that his friends had planned for months as a graduation present to themselves. And for the first time in as long as he could remember, he told his grandparents that he wouldn't be working in the deli that summer. That Sunday dinner when he announced his plans to the extended family had been surreal. The protection of company had tamped his father's reaction down to a dull, angry glare; but his mother had burst into tears at the sudden news of him leaving early.

Why did he have to leave so soon? What about the summer and his friends? What was so urgent? Why couldn't he wait till September to leave for college? Everyone else's kids were. He spent that evening, and the entire week that followed, repeating his assurances—Professor Pennington had already arranged a summer job for him on campus, his room and board were included while he worked, he was already assigned to a large crew of freshmen that were all coming early, he wouldn't be alone. There were lots of new people to meet.

For most of his family and friends, the assurances slowly took root and soothed the shock of his early departure. But Luka focused the majority of his time preparing for the imminent blowout with his father. The tension in the house was palpable, like an invisible rope pulled taut around the throats of the family, choking them into silence at every dinner, every breakfast, anytime they were together. Luka had prepared his facts carefully and had thought and re-thought the counter-arguments; all that he would say to answer his father's objections down to the last detail. He knew how he would earn his money, where he would live, his study program for the first year, his advisors, the work crew supervisor—he had contacted them all; he was prepared for the coming eruption.

But more importantly, Luka kept the actual facts well hidden: that the summer crews didn't show up until early August; that he had worked frantically with Professor Pennington to find the only job he could—working with one of the private campus contractors, remodeling the dormitories; that not until the very last minute had he gotten approval to stay in the freshman dorms while they were being remodeled, not that lack of permission would have stopped him from leaving Minnesota.

But in the end, the confrontation never came. He and his father went to opposite corners of their lives and pushed their joint conflict down into the shadows. At first Luka was relieved at the realization that he was free to leave. But in the end he was even angrier, knowing how much was unspoken, but having no desire to force the issue open for fear it might somehow stop his leaving. Like a gaping wound left untended, never completely healing; this, like the rest of his dealings with his father, wouldn't mend properly. It would forever leave a disfiguring scar behind.

Luka laid low on the top of the hill and watched the checkpoint at Ettenheim through his binoculars. He had hoped to ditch the car several klicks south of here on the drive up, somewhere more remote and safe, and then head into the hills on foot, paralleling the road. But seeing Erik's struggle out of the boardinghouse had changed that plan. They would now have to get as close to Ettenheim as possible, minimize the hiking, start slower.

They had surreptitiously approached along a dirt road that snaked its way along the perimeter of several farms and had finally ditched the car in a grove of overgrown scrub oak. This was as close as they dared get to the checkpoint by car, still at least twenty kilometers away from Haslach.

The checkpoint at Ettenheim appeared at first glance to be out of place, simple, and set low along a lone two-lane road in the trough of a long, shallow valley, appearing out of the way and innocent. But in reality the checkpoint was ideally placed and well utilized. Anyone entering the valley was observed early from the checkpoint, approaching for a full kilometer in any direction. If you weren't supposed to be there, you didn't dare turn around; the checkpoint guards would quickly radio ahead to Seschmal to the south, or Ettenheim to the north, and you were caught either way. Luka had passed through the checkpoint many times over the years, and the place had always given him the creeps, as it was designed to do.

Observing from the low hillock, Luka watched German convoys moving through the valley, heading toward Ettenheim. More than likely their final destination was the front that was now advancing on Haslach that Jack had told him about. There was a steady stream of men and equipment; he and Erik would have to be very careful crossing the main highway north and on into the valley. They would have to wait for nightfall.

Luka slid back down the hill to rejoin Erik, hidden in the scrub oak of the little ravine. Erik was seated on the bumper of the car, busy fumbling with the straps of the old canvas backpack that Luka had loaned him. Luka had packed it lightly, in hopes that Erik could ease back into hiking quickly, but the bigger worry was Erik's injuries. Even though Doctor Dietr had tended to him for five days, the shrapnel wound on Erik's leg looked swollen and angry, and in addition he had the recently dislocated shoulder and likely concussion. Luka had serious doubts about bringing Erik along.

"How do you feel?" Luka asked.

"Good. I took one of the pain pills you stole. My leg feels a lot better. It's mostly my shoulder that hurts, but that won't stop me from walking."

"Listen..." Luka started.

But Erik quickly interrupted him, "Forget it! I know what you're going to say, but I'm coming with you."

"I can get in and out of there much faster than we both can together, three days at most, and then I'll be back. I have a place I can hide you on the far side of Ettenheim; it's close, and it's stocked with provisions. You would be a whole lot safer there, away from the front. You can rest up. I'll find the warehouse, call in the evacuation, and then come back and get you."

Erik stopped adjusting the pack and stared straight at Luka, "And what if you don't?"

They stared at each other in silence for several minutes before Erik continued, "The German deserter gets you in. Then you, the doctor and the colonel all take off with the paintings. Why come back for me? Why would you risk that?"

Erik stared back, waiting for an answer. "Yeah right..." he finally mumbled, and went back to adjusting the pack.

Luka stood in silence. He continued staring back, but he didn't have an answer. Erik was right. Since leaving the boardinghouse, Luka had quickly identified the tension that traveling with his newfound companion raised. It reminded him of sitting on the porch in Minnesota with his father. But now he realized the unease went both ways— neither one trusted the other.

Erik stopped again, looking up to stare Luka in the eyes. "And I want my painting. MY painting, of my life, they promised it to me. I don't want it to end up on some truck halfway across France and into Allied territory where I'll never see it again."

Luka sighed and stood. "It's getting late," he muttered. "Let's at least get through this ravine, it leads to a creek and small bridge that'll take us under the road. We can move slowly get used to the packs."

"Fine," Erik answered without looking up.

"We have to wait for nightfall to cross under. There are troops traveling north, we just have to hope they're staying on the main roads and out of the valley. The mortar fire seems to be several kilometers west yet, and the weather is supposed to hold for the next few days. We should be alright."

Erik grimaced as he stood, shouldering the backpack. Luka could see the pain he tried his best to hide as he hobbled down the ravine and into the bushes.

He quickly did the math—together, it would be at least three days just to get there, maybe four; another day to get inside the warehouse and verify the paintings, another to make contact and wait for the smuggler's transport he had hastily arranged; six days total, possibly more! They would be lucky to get in and out before Haslach was overrun. He shook his head slowly in disgust.

As Luka watched Erik disappear into the undergrowth ahead, a pang of regret rose in him, and not for the first time that day. It was still possible to turn back, run for the hidden car, and make it back to Trier before nightfall, radio Jack and wait in the bunker for pickup. It wouldn't be hard to make up a story, how Erik had escaped and Luka had tracked him down before radioing in.

But that would mean the end of anything that waited for him to discover in Haslach. Jack would have him out of Germany by morning, Haslach would be overrun, and it definitely meant having to kill Erik and leave him here in the scrub hidden outside of Ettenheim, so that he couldn't talk to anyone else. Luka could still get away clean.

He repeated the calming ritual he had quickly grown into over the last twenty-four hours, lifting the scrap of painting Erik had brought him out of his pocket and let it work its wonder on him again. The details of the square in Trier; with him, Erik and Claudia perfectly depicted, before it had even happened. It tugged at him again, pulled him forward with the need to see thousands of scenes just like this one, and to find out how this was even possible.

Luka picked up his pack and headed into the brush after Erik.

Chapter 19

Work started early on the summer dorm renovations. The contracting crew showed up by 6 a.m. to avoid working in the heat of the afternoon. The work was physical and demanding. One day it might be running a floor sander—starting at one end of a long hallway in the morning and finishing at the other by afternoon. Another would be tearing out desks and display cases from the chemistry lab, spending all day bent over pulling nailed fixtures up with claw hammers and crowbars.

The foreman quickly learned that he could give Luka a task in the morning, and by afternoon he would come back to find it done, and done right. There was no need to watch over him. The majority of the crew came and went quickly that summer, constantly needing to be replaced, temp laborers that would show up for a day or two, a week at most, and then move on to something else that paid better or was less strenuous.

But Luka loved the absent-mindedness of it all; no one to placate, no one to worry about what they were thinking of him, what they wanted from him. At first the other workers tried to talk him into slowing down, taking more breaks; no need to hurry and rush through the day—after all, he was making the rest of them look bad! But after a week, they gave up on him and left him to his solo labors.

Luka squatted low on the hill in the haze of the afternoon watching both sides of the valley for movement. They had crossed under the small road leading to the checkpoint with relative ease, but as the dead of night fell, when they could have made the best progress, Erik slowed to a crawl, wincing in pain; and despite Luka carrying both packs, Erik had to stop well before morning. They had only reached the valley on the far side of Ettenheim. To the north ahead still lay the main highway dotted with convoys of troops headed west. Luka had planned to cross the main highway farther north during the early hours before morning, but in the end it wasn't going to happen, and now an extra day had been tacked on to their hike. It would be late into tomorrow night before they could even attempt to cross the highway, when the convoys were at a lull.

The day had quickly grown hot and humid, so Luka found a dense growth of pine and left Erik there to sleep in the shade and relative cool of a bed of pine straw. Then, climbing back up to the top of the hill, he baked in the afternoon sun, watching and planning, the heat serving to make him angrier as he mentally beat himself up.

They were both wanted men now. The courier would have immediately contacted Jack to let him know that Luka had missed their rendezvous. Jack's worst fears would now be confirmed; and Luka's name, his fake German papers, his description, and his photos would have been leaked to every German constable and radioed to every Allied commander in this sector. He was now in the worst of all possible situations: he was a mole, a double-agent, hunted by both sides.

And someone certainly had gotten to the doctor by now—either one of Jack's goons or the SS. Erik's description would be at every checkpoint throughout Bavaria.

"Biggest mistake you'll ever make." The phrase replayed back to him at every dark crevasse in his current situation. His father's admonition had been expressed at his desire to become an artist, but in reflection Luka wondered if the missive had been given to him to file away and pull out whenever the situation fit. His subconscious had taken it to heart.

As evening approached, Luka fingered his future, the piece of painting in his pocket. Even though he couldn't see it, its presence in his hand was reassuring, something to move forward towards. As he watched the valley below, he gingerly felt the thin lines of dried oil rising in relief from the canvas. Maybe this ridge he was following with his finger was Claudia's dark hair, or maybe it was his hand on the railing as he stood in shock, staring across the square at Erik's advance.

How this painting was possible, he had no idea—but he wanted to know what could have created this kind of wonder. He wanted to see it for himself.

Chapter 20

On the other side of the campus, at the Liberal Arts College, Professor Pennington had stayed on during the early weeks of June to watch over the Fine Arts Lab expansion, knocking out two walls of adjoining classrooms and adding on a much needed, expanded storage locker. Luka spent all his free afternoons and evenings that June helping the professor do whatever needed to be done: move supplies, pack or unpack boxes, tear down equipment, set up equipment. He even rebuilt an old metal lathe that had sat idle, donated to the school ten years prior.

The expansion was completed ahead of schedule and under budget thanks in large part to Luka's free labor. In appreciation, the professor had handed the keys of the lab over to Luka for the remainder of the summer, his only two instructions being: pay for your own materials, and don't break anything.

And now his afternoons were exquisite. As soon as work ended in the early afternoon, Luka would jog the two miles across campus, unlock the lab, and immerse himself in creation. It was utter freedom, with time to explore. Clays, paints, stone and mortar, charcoals, metal facings, enamels, plastics and resins, laminates. He tried brushes, conte, nib, palette knifes, adhesives, propane torches; applying them to canvas, wood, muslin, even cinder-block wall. He was free to investigate all types of styles and techniques; frescos, murals, quadratura, busts, rosemaling... the combinations were endless. Some blends of style and material led to disgusting messes, but Luka didn't care; he learned by experiment what material worked with what medium, and in what style, simply by trying it, the oldest and deepest form of art education.

Luka forced himself to delve into the variety of treasures in the lab, but he would always come back to sculpting as his first love. Sometimes he used discarded chunks of limestone or porphyry. But wanting to save his money, and having to cover his own expenses and materials, Luka more and more drifted back to clay and castings.

Professor Pennington dropped in from time to time in the evenings to check on him and to see his results. Sometimes he would offer direction, other times just watch and enjoy the unbridled exploration, always bringing along with him a six-pack of Pabst Blue Ribbon beer and a pizza. He and Luka would eat and talk art, sometimes late into the night. Soon the professor had Luka reading art publications to discover new directions; *Art Journal CAA*, *Minotaure*, and *Frieze* began collecting in neat, tall stacks next to his mattress on the floor of his dorm room.

Surely this was heaven!

Luka let Erik rest until after midnight, in hopes that he would regain some strength, and to catch the low point of traffic crossing the highway ahead. Together they followed the hilltop meadow they were on until it began sloping down to the highway and the stream cutting through the forest below. There was only one stretch of the highway within three klicks either way that offered the bend in the road Luka wanted, a broad sweeping arc through at least one-hundred-thirty degrees, so that oncoming headlights only briefly illuminated any single portion of the road as trucks turned through the curve.

This was the least risky point to cross the highway, but unfortunately the steepest embankments flanked both sides. Luka tried to find the best way possible for Erik to get down the steep slope, but the reality was there was no easy way down. In the end he took both packs and Erik tried scooting down the hill that ended streamside beside the highway.

Scooting along on his butt jarred Erik's leg, and the stream crossing proved no easier. He couldn't balance well on the rocks and continually slipped into the water. By the time they had finally crossed and reached the near edge of the highway he was in pain again, and they hadn't even traveled two kilometers yet.

Erik rested, pressed prone into the low grassy bank of the highway while Luka scouted ahead to find the best way up the embankment on the opposite side. The hour had paid off, the intervals between oncoming trucks had grown to several minutes. Luka returned from his scouting and whispered, "I see a small drainage on the other side about half a kilometer further that leads up the other bank. We cross here, drop low into the culvert on the other side, follow the road around and then head up the drainage into the forest. It's the most gradual way I can see up."

"Good," Erik answered, tentatively.

"Wait for me to start, and stay low until then. I'll cross first, you follow. Stay exactly in my path. Move cautiously but as quickly as you can. I'll try not to move too fast. And watch out for the raised median. Alright?"

Erik nodded.

Luka moved up the embankment to the lip of the highway, pressed flat against the grass. In the distance a rumble could be heard rounding the far bend, coming their way. A convoy of heavy supply trucks came into view, moving slowly and steadily along. Three in all, towing mortar cannons behind.

Luka waited until the third truck was alongside, turned, and nodded to Erik, who nodded back.

As the last truck cleared the apex of the bend, Luka lifted himself smoothly off the grass and began a steady jog across the highway. He glanced back briefly to confirm Erik was following, cut a straight line across the asphalt, across the median, across the far lane, and then down the embankment. He turned and watched. Erik was loping across, more upright and stiff than Luka would have liked, but at the moment all he wished for was speed out of Erik. "Just get across," he mumbled.

Erik's slow awkward gait was painful to watch, but he made steady progress. Then just as he was leaving the roadway for the safety of the gulley, Luka heard a loud "HALT" come from the far side of the road.

He looked intently for the source of the shout but couldn't find it. Erik kept coming and dove for the safety of the ditch. And then, gunfire, three rifle shots in quick succession! Luka heard the whiz of the last bullet as it flew overhead, the muzzle flash finally giving away the location. A German soldier was jogging up the opposite side of the road, headed for the bend in the highway they had just left. He yelled again, "HALT. DON'T MOVE!" then stopped and raised his rifle, pointed at where Erik had just disappeared from the road. Another shot rang out and zipped past just over where Erik lay in the culvert.

"Go!" Luka whispered to Erik and pushed him off in the direction of the drainage ahead. "Stay low, I'm right behind you."

Erik began a hobble-run crouched low along the bottom of the ditch. Luka reached around into the covering flap of his pack and pulled out the loaded Luger.

The soldier across the road was yelling over his shoulder now, "OVER HERE, I NEED HELP! SOMEONE SNEAKING ACROSS THE HIGHWAY!" And now he was running toward them, crossing the highway. Luka heard the sound of his boots landing hollow on the asphalt.

"Damn," Luka whispered to himself. "Keep going!" he whispered hoarsely to Erik. "Whatever you do, don't stop, and don't turn around." And then Luka stopped, crouched even lower in the culvert, back-stepped ten paces, snapped the safety from the Luger, and waited.

He could hear the soldier's footsteps getting close as he watched Erik disappear around the far bend of the ditch.

"YOU...HALT. HALT OR I'LL SHOOT," the soldier yelled as he crossed the last of the roadway and dropped into the ditch right where Erik had entered, just ahead of Luka. Luka raised the revolver smoothly, arm outstretched, and fired once at the back of the soldier's head.

The soldier's arms splayed outwards in a sudden, violent spread eagle, as he involuntarily tossed the rifle and hit the bottom of the ditch face first. Luka stood and fired again into the soldier's back. The soldier jerked but made no more sounds.

Luka crouched down to retrieve the rifle, opened the breech, and expelled the smoking, empty shell. He patted the dead soldier up and down until he found two bandoliers of ammunition, stuffing them into his backpack. He stopped momentarily, staying low, to look and listen, but could hear nothing else. And then he took off, around the bend after Erik, deftly slinging the rifle over his shoulder and onto his back as he ran.

Around the next bend he could see Erik had started up the drainage; he was slipping on damp rocks, trying to climb, grimacing as he went.

Luka quickly closed the distance between them, and then scrambled up the first few feet until he met Erik's progress. He shoved his hand hard into Erik's butt, "MOVE!"

"What happened?" Erik called back.

"JUST MOVE!" Luka growled in response, pushing harder.

It was an excruciating climb for both of them, Luka pushing Erik with one hand from below, forcing him to scramble up the slippery climb, Erik stumbling and moaning in pain more than once as his leg gave out beneath the added pressure. They collapsed near the top, panting and sweating, where the little drainage finally flattened out.

After only a few seconds Luka stood and ran along the perimeter of the ridge, back to the east above the bend in the road.

"Where are you going?" Erik asked after him.

Luka turned and waved his arm sharply in rebuke, finger to his mouth.

He disappeared into the darkness, leaving Erik flat on his back, lungs on fire, trying desperately to catch his breath.

Luka found what he had been hoping for: a vantage point high above the bend in the highway. From this elevation he could clearly see the small squad of soldiers and vehicles parked on the unmarked dirt turnoff, not seventy meters from where they had first slid down the embankment to meet the stream. It's amazing they hadn't been discovered sooner.

On the near side, crouched in the culvert, a group of soldiers and officers stood examining the body of their now dead comrade. The hair on the back of Luka's neck stood on end. Their journey had just grown far more severe, and deadly.

After much discussion a dark-suited officer pointed, and three soldiers took off toward the drainage, the way he and Erik had just escaped.

Erik's leg throbbed in pain in regular pulses, like a metronome following the too rapid beating of his heart. He tried to calm down, relax. He pulled himself up, back propped against a large rock, and forced some deep breaths. That and some quick sips from his canteen and he began to calm down. The pain in his leg subsided and grew less sharp.

Erik tried to concentrate and listen, to see if he could hear anything on the blowing night wind. And then abruptly, Luka appeared ahead, breaking through a grove of dark trees. The suddenness of it startled Erik. Luka moved swiftly, like a deer through the night. He came up quietly and dropped to his knees, quickly flinging off his backpack and opening it.

Luka whispered quietly between pants, "We're not done yet. We have to keep moving."

Erik shook his head in protest.

"We're being hunted. At least three more soldiers."

Luka opened the Luger, checked and reloaded it, cocked it, reset the safety, then replaced it in the backpack. He took a quick sip of his own canteen, closed and stowed it, stood and shouldered his backpack, then offered an arm to pull Erik up.

"Come on."

"I don't think I..." Erik started.

"Listen," Luka dropped to eye-level to face Erik directly. "If they catch us, we're dead. I killed a man back there, or he would have killed you. Now they're coming for us. Do you understand? If we don't move now, we die. It's that simple."

Luka stood, pulled Erik to his feet, and pushed him forward without waiting for a response.

Erik stumbled, pain shooting up his leg, but kept moving. He slung the pack still in his hand onto his shoulders and began hobbling as fast as his leg would allow him. Keeping his leg straight and stiff, the pain wasn't quite so bad, but he couldn't see what his foot was landing on: grass, dirt, stone, stump—and some of the steps were jarring and resonated up into his hip.

Luka continued to push him from behind, urging him forward. "Can you go any faster?"

But when Erik bent his leg to try to jog, the pain was far worse. Through gritted teeth he shook his head, pulled up, and managed, "No, stop pushing me!"

On they went into the cover of the forest. Their progress was slow, but a full moon was up, and the night sky was clear, with a crosswind blowing light and steady along the top of the ridge. Luka could see several meters ahead and could easily make out the line of hills that led north into the Nekar and on to Haslach. Their path was gradual and rolling, with sparse trees along the sloping ridge tops.

"Ow! This really hurts." Erik suddenly straightened and slowed.

"You're not moving fast enough, they'll catch us at this pace." Luka pushed again, urging Erik along.

"I can't go any faster!" Erik pulled up and stopped.

"Shit!" Luka hissed.

Luka paced back and forth, trying to figure out what to do next. They were standing on a broad limestone cap at the top of a sloping hill.

"It's the rock we're on that's hurting your leg. We'll be back on dirt just ahead."

"No," Erik insisted. He was doubled-over, panting and grimacing. "The pain is too much. I swear I'm going to pass out. I need a minute."

Luka stared back and forth along their path for something that could help.

Then he walked to the edge of the limestone cap and laid down, head disappearing over the western lip. He pushed himself back up on his hands. "Alright, here's what we're doing" he announced.

Chapter 21

During the peak of summer break, Luka would be at the arts lab by three-thirty, and work until eight-thirty or nine before exhaustion finally overtook him. The first few weeks, he would spend the early part of the evening trying to cool the lab off, to get away from the heat of summer. But Luka discovered one luscious July evening that the best way for him to cool off was to immerse his hands and arms into a mound of clay. Bring the ache, the sweat, the exhaustion, and let the fresh, wet earth take over; it seemed to know what to do with him. Slowly the day would be drawn out of him like a soothing balm. Repeatedly gripping the brown mass could release even the worst vibrations of the floor buffer. Any cuts he might have taken from a day of pulling up boards and nails seemed to relieve, and even begin to heal, in the balm of the healing clay.

What was most amazing was how the mud could speak to him. In some ethereal way, he could reach deep in the clay, relax his mind, and as he kneaded it, like a fine pastry, the medium seemed to speak to him, to tell him what was hidden inside that day, waiting to be extracted. The clay seemed to want Luka as he much as he needed the clay.

It took all of Luka's patience and persistence to get Erik onto the recessed ledge that hung below the limestone cap. They had to back-track to the beginning of the stone exposure, and with Luka leading, inch along the exposed face of the ledge out to the middle, where there was room to move, hidden under the ridge above.

After sitting Erik down against the back of the stone ledge Luka explained, "Stay here, and try to keep as quiet as you can. You have water and food; try to use it sparingly. Keep your body still, slow your processes down, let your leg rest. Stay wrapped up at night—you'll be cold out here on the rocks. Nights are the worst. Hopefully it stays dry."

"I don't understand."

Luka gave Erik a grave look. "Those soldiers will be on us shortly, probably within the next hour. If they're good and they have a tracker, we're dead at the pace we've been moving. I believe they only saw you, they don't know I'm with you. Maybe I can lead them away." Luka stood to leave.

Erik started to shake his head.

"It's the only thing I can think of," he added, matter-of-factly. "Now, listen carefully. If I'm not back in two days, I'm dead, and you're on your own."

"No," Erik whispered back, stunned.

Luka paused, not knowing how to respond. "I'm sorry," he finally managed, and then he was off, scrambling back across the narrow ridge and into the night the way they had come.

Four hundred meters back, Luka found the meadow he had remembered crossing, a large open glade that sloped slowly away to the west and east, covered with wild buffalo grass. From the center of the meadow, the path they had followed was up and over a very gradual rise. Luka snapped a long branch of pine bow filled with fresh evergreen needles and then backed down the path into the center of the meadow, sweeping over their tracks as he went, attempting to fluff up the grass as much as possible.

In the center of the meadow Luka stopped to inspect his work. Crouching low, and searching for it, broken blades of grass from their boot steps were still visible leading up and to the north. But standing, at night, with the steady wind waving the long grass back and forth, the path they had traveled was hard to discern.

Luka could still see it, but it would have to be enough. He was out of time; he would just have to hope they didn't have an experienced tracker in the team and that the soldiers would follow the most obvious clues. Luka began hobbling across the meadow, imitating Erik's bad gait, but at twice the speed. First heading northeast, and then turning east, a great shallow arc leading away from the ridge where Erik was hiding. As he left the meadow and re-entered the forest, Luka made sure to snap a few small tree limbs.

Luka kept up the hobbling gait for well over an hour, until his hip was sore from the extended pounding. Just as dawn was drawing a hint of purple across the horizon in front of him, the dense forest gave way to an open meadow bisected by a small meandering stream. Luka hobbled across, making sure to stop and crouch at the stream to leave footprints in the soft mud.

In the forest on the far eastern side of the meadow, Luka spied a large lodgepole pine with a split trunk and a low canopy of branches that held a heavy spray of fresh spring needles and cones. It was at least thirty meters away from the path he was cutting, a good vantage point. He stopped long enough to double-check his bearings against the map, and to replenish with some water and deer jerky; then he continued on east.

After another hour, with dawn breaking full, Luka found what he was looking for. On the top of a broad rise lay an expanse of dry meadow that hadn't seen enough rain to spring into flower yet. As he reached the far end he turned, and began jogging in great crisscrossing circles around the edge of the hard dry scrabble. When he was finally satisfied with the confusion of tracks he turned back west and began jogging a great arc back to the lodgepole pine.

Erik spent the remainder of the night propped with his back against the cold chalk wall at the back of the recess. Now that he was no longer running, the cold quickly overtook him, and the rock floor and backrest only amplified the chill. He was afraid to sleep, waking often; and when he dozed he would suddenly jerk awake, convinced he had heard something on the ledge above him.

The cold and solitude of the night, then pain in his arm and leg, and his dire surroundings took Erik back to his desertion just weeks before, and the desperateness he now felt flooded over him. He wept quietly as the morning slowly approached from behind. The night gave way to sunrise only begrudgingly. His shelter faced west onto the shallow valley below, and the relief of dawn wasn't obvious until it was well underway.

Chapter 22

It was close to noon by the time Luka's circling led back to the big lodgepole pine. His feet were aching, his body exhausted. With a last push, he climbed into the saddle of the big split trunk and hung his backpack on a solid knot, hidden in the dense spray of pine needles.

From his vantage point, Luka scanned the far side of the valley for any sign of movement. He had identified three possibilities: 1) they were ordinary soldiers and would follow his tracks; 2) there was a professional among them and they could be tracking either him or Erik, or worse, both; or 3) they had given up the search during the night.

He had hoped to see the soldiers appear early. It would mean they were following the most obvious tracks, his. The longer they took to follow, the more likely they were being led by an experienced, methodical tracker, or that they had discovered Erik.

Luka stared into his binoculars, searching for movement at the far side of the meadow. Concentrating into the lenses he saw in slow motion as the soldier dropped into the culvert ahead of him, then his own hand reaching into view, pointing the Luger at the back of the soldier's head. Time slowed to a crawl, and Luka saw the gun kick, smoke jetting from the muzzle, the slug of lead leaving the barrel, headed straight to the man's head to end his life. Time froze to a halt in his memory, like a perfect little painting.

Luka dropped the binoculars to shake the image away. He was daydreaming due to lack of sleep. It had happened before on long overnights. But now his hands were shaking too, and that was new.

He rubbed his hands, trying to shake the cold of the night from them despite the sun beating down through the branches. Luka shook his head, trying again to clear the memory, then raised the binoculars to see only a doe and fawn, headed cautiously to the stream for a drink.

He lowered the binoculars, rubbed his eyes, and reached into his backpack for something to eat. As he ate a slice of cheese wrapped in lunchmeat, his mind wandered...

The south Texas heat and the middle of August combined to make the Special Forces Training School miserable. The bald cypress grove spread overhead like the broad spread fingers of sleeping giants, a dome above his path that concentrated the mid-day heat, creating one giant outdoor sauna that stretched in all directions for miles. Sweat ran off every inch of his body, into his face, down his back, into the crack of his ass. His legs and feet were continually soaked from crouching in the swamp. They itched intensely, probably from jungle rot, and he was convinced that when he could finally walk out, he would have permanent blisters.

Luka shook his head, trying to focus, walk a steady pace, making sure to listen between movements, recounting all the classroom lessons he had absorbed over the last several weeks. It was starting to come more naturally; the individual exercises were gelling into a whole that made sense; pistol ready, pointed ahead, clearing the area surrounding, slowly, steadily, searching for the enemy.

Below in the mud he spied a large water moccasin crossing his path, and paused to let it move on. That's when he heard the wet "thup" of boots dropping behind him into the mud. Simultaneously he felt the cold steel barrel pressed against his head.

"Noooo," he moaned.

"Oh, yeah, Plebe...again. You haven't cleared above for the last thirty minutes, HAVE YOU?"

Luka didn't answer, he just shook his head slowly in disgust. Three pairs of senior marauders' arms grabbed his shoulders and back, threw the rough burlap sack over his head, then shoved him down hard into the muck. He felt the hot, dank breath of a marauder in his ear as he growled, "Third time this week, Plebe, that's a washout."

"NO!" Luka yelled.

"I'm not asking...you don't call it, Grunt. I DO!" he shouted in Luka's ear.

"NO!"

The men on top of him laughed.

"NO!" he yelled back, even louder.

"You sure?"

Luka didn't answer, and he didn't fight.

"What'll it be, then?"

"I'M NOT OUT!"

There was a long pause filled with more laughter. Then he was yanked violently to his feet. "Alright...THEN RUN, PUKE!" came the answer, followed by a swift kick to his back.

The thought of the jog back to base made his stomach turn. They had to be at least three miles out, back through the heat and mud, at full run, hands tied behind his back, gunny sack pulled snug over his head, flanked by two marauders that would harass and yell at him in both ears the whole way, men that specialized in humiliation.

"You're not just a failure, YOU'RE DEAD...You know the worst part, you sack of monkey shit? It ain't that your lily-white ass is dead, I could care less...the worst part is you blew everyone else's cover...you got teammates killed because YOU CAN'T FUNCTION OUT HERE...The SS will feed you to the pigs...nice fat German pigs raised on American MAGGOTS LIKE YOU...you raise incompetence to an art form..."

And on and on and on; but that wasn't the worst part. The worst would come in meeting with the chief instructor in debrief afterward. The first month, the CI had just screamed in every recruit's face until the most obvious washouts gave up and left. But in the last week his tone had shifted and his arguments were logical.

"Don't listen to the marauders, Luka, there's no shame in washing out from here. You've already passed Officer's Training, be happy with that. For every class of one-hundred recruits, only three make it to the end out here. Are you in that top three percent, Luka? Really, be honest with yourself. The people coming out of this training have to have the instincts of a killer, and maybe you just don't have it. You need to ask yourself that, and be honest with the answer, you'll be much happier in the end."

But Luka was determined to endure.

Then came the day in early September when he was the first recruit in his class to make it through the course. He had stayed out for two days and nights crouched low in the hollow of a dead cypress trunk out of sheer determination. After two hours he had horrible leg cramps, but he willed himself past it. At night he found himself hallucinating, waking up sure he had shouted in his sleep, but he trusted himself and stayed silent.

He knew there was a marauder close; something just didn't feel right in the swamp. And in the end the marauder had finally moved, come down from his tree to cross to a new position, and Luka had him. He moved smoothly and quietly out of his hiding place in the tree trunk to meet the marauder's back, raised his pistol, and he could clearly see the horror of the bullet entering the back of the German soldier's head, his nervous system react with a final burst of electricity, jolting the soldier's arms stiff, body tightening in complete shock, as he fell to the ditch face first, dead.

Luka snapped awake, almost falling from the notch. He rocked back and forth, trying to shake off the dream, and finally acknowledged the gravity of what was pulling on him. The German soldier chasing them down the highway was the first person he had killed. He was supposed to have the instincts of a killer—it was an instinct necessary to be a good spy, and it was required in war. But what he was now involved in, what he was chasing with Erik, was no longer war. He had managed to make it through all of his spy missions without having to kill a single person; nut now Luka was off the grid, and his mission had been officially terminated. He hadn't been threatened, his life wasn't in danger when he pulled the trigger.

No, he tried to protest in response to his realization, to stop it from coming.

But his conscience knew the truth now. He had killed the soldier to make sure they both reached the warehouse together, so that they could both discover how a stranger's life could be captured in a painting, and his future foretold. He could have let the soldier kill Erik and continue on alone. It would have been much easier, in fact.

As Luka's body began to rack with sobs, he could swear he heard the wind in the trees whisper low, "Biggest mistake you'll ever make."

Chapter 23

Fall finally arrived and brought with it a dramatic change to the campus. Luka "officially" moved into the freshman dorm after being assigned a smaller, standard room on the third floor, whereupon he was united with his roommate for the year—Doug, a six-foot, gangly business arts major from Maryland. Doug's family was steeped in money, and he carried on an endless monologue on how despite the freshman rules, his mother would get him out of this stinking dorm and into an off-campus house; either that or which fraternity he would be pledging.

Simultaneously the Arts College swung into preparation for the approaching school year. The fall prep crews now spent their days setting up classrooms, and the afternoons were filled with faculty meetings. Luka's free access to the arts lab was retracted, as a schedule for the coming year was drawn up; and Professor Pennington grew scarce as he went about the preparations of a normal load of courses and scheduled office hours.

The biggest shock for Luka came as freshman classes started. Surrounded by the best and brightest, Luka quickly found himself tossed into an unspoken competition to stand out, to be noticed and unique. It was a quality he had observed in others but had never cultivated for himself; his natural artistic talents had always let him stand out against the other high-school students in his little corner of Minnesota. But here, thrown into the concentration of the arts college, to be good at your craft, to be creative, was no longer enough. Luka was surrounded by the finest art students from across the land; and as the freshman shock of the new environment gave way to routine, he became more and more aware of a trait that the standouts had and that he didn't. It was there, on the tip of his tongue, but it remained unnamed, just out of reach.

It was early afternoon before a group of soldiers finally emerged through the grove of trees to the west, entering the open meadow. They moved slowly, deliberately, following his tracks into the small meadow headed toward the stream. Three were German soldiers in regular fatigues, carrying packs and sniper rifles, the same dress as the soldier he had killed. But on either end of this group, leading and trailing, were a pair of SS officers. Luka could clearly see the black double-lightning-bolt shoulder patches through his binoculars. The initial search party must have circled back early in the morning after losing the trail, and had gone back to get more experienced men. Luka's pulse began to race.

He watched intently through the binoculars as the group eventually reached the stream, where the lead officer stopped and crouched, examining the heavy boot prints Luka had left in the mud. After a brief discussion the officer stood and slowly walked upstream along the bank, carefully examining the stream bed as he went. The man was thorough, an experienced tracker, good enough to suspect the heavy footprints might be a decoy, that his prey's true route of escape could be through the water, where tracks and scent were easily lost.

"Damn," Luka whispered. He knew this would now be much more difficult than he had hoped for. He lowered the binoculars, and without taking his eyes off the tracking party, he began carefully repacking, then brought the rifle around into his lap. He gently clicked in a bandolier and quietly cocked the weapon.

The tracking party eventually crossed the little stream and headed to the east side of the meadow, still following his tracks. Gradually they moved into the trees alongside him.

Luka synched the strap of the rifle tight against his forearm and targeted the leading SS officer. Through the rifle's scope he lined the officer's head into the fine crosshairs. In the sight the man appeared deliberate, purposeful. The officer deftly followed Luka's tracks through the dense clump of trees and on up the small rise of hill.

Luka lowered the gun and watched as the group slowly proceeded out of sight, following his tracks further east.

Chapter 24

Table after table filled the grand ballroom of the Albany Hilton. Sculptures, obelisks, paintings, mobiles, pottery, and glassworks filled the tables, some sharp and domineering, others subtle and subdued. The majority of tables were flanked by a nervous art student dressed in either a suit and tie or a long dress. The fall semester exhibition was in full swing, and every underclass art major was expected to show his or her best semester works surrounding a theme. The exhibition was not only scrutinized and judged by the arts faculty; it was widely known that gallery owners from around the state frequented the biannual event to begin to identify and start tracking new talent.

Luka expectantly treated the evening the same way he had wanted the Arts College to treat him. He was enrolled in a meritocracy, and his works would speak for themselves. The clay pieces he had chosen to display would cause onlookers to stop, even pull some in for a closer look. But after that, Luka was lost—he would sometimes politely ask "Can I answer any questions for you?" But beyond that, he didn't try to engage his audience, or even understand why he needed to.

Across the way, Luka could distinctly hear Michelle's shrill voice rising above the dull conversation roar that defined the room. A loud-mouthed junior from Manhattan, Luka considered her work half-rate and uninspired. She was extolling the virtues of iridium powder blown onto hot blown glass to a group of onlookers that Luka didn't recognize. He slowly wandered closer to better observe.

"...yes, that's true. But I'm unique because I'm applying it straight from the furnace, while the glass is still molten, even before the color has been gathered. See here..."

She grabbed a large glass monstrosity from the table beside her. It was a twisted ribbon of forest-green-and-white striped taffy wrapped in clear glass that had been turned and bent back on itself into an enormous knot, until it resembled nothing in particular. She held it too high, so that the whole room would notice it.

"You see...I turned the furnace down to fifteen hundred degrees for this piece, much lower than recommended for standard art glass, spraying the iridium directly after the first gather. The lower temperature of the glass forces chemicals in the spray to burn off at different rates, leaving a very unique hue."

Luka didn't know if her speech was even remotely accurate, but he recognized that it made for good theater. From the edge, he watched the crowd mutter and stare closely at the piece of abstract artwork she held high. Off to one side he noted Professors Pennington and Rashard watching the commotion; conversing back and forth, laughing, and then nodding and smiling.

This was argument by intimidation. You either agreed and went along with the aesthete or you were excluded. And then Luka heard the voice in his head again, "Biggest mistake you'll ever make," and a sickening feeling pulled at the pit of his stomach. What was it that he didn't understand here?

Luka crossed the large glade of buffalo grass quickly, as soon as the search party was out of sight. He reached Erik's hiding place in the chalk cliffs by dusk. He wanted desperately to move, to put some distance between themselves, the highway, and the tracking party; but a full day of running and lack of sleep claimed their toll, and Luka had to rest for a few hours on the chalk ledge while Erik held guard listening above.

They started out again toward Haslach well after midnight, and Luka was hugely disappointed to find out that Erik's leg was little better. Even with twenty-four hours of rest Erik limped gingerly, grimacing with each step, and they made slow progress.

Chapter 25

By the end of his freshman year, Luka had learned how to manage his time, how to balance studying and work. He found the equilibrium that is much of the focus of a first year at college, and he even developed a social life. But his art grew into a struggle. His works were considered good, consistently in the upper half of the class, but he couldn't find a way to make them prominent, attract attention. No matter how hard he tried, it wouldn't come from extra studying; it seemed to flow from a place of confidence that he couldn't quite cultivate. Something that had once been the focus of his life, that had been easy and wonderful, his center, was now work, difficult; it demanded a new relationship with him, and Luka couldn't find how to both love it and work at it simultaneously.

There were other students, however, that did stand out, and they seemed to do it with an ease that was unsettling. It was a quality Luka secretly dubbed "brass balls." Those that had "brass balls" would dive into their art, without even considering if the idea they followed was worth pursuing. Most often the results would be crap, very rarely the outcome was genius; but what seemed to be most important— "brass balls" drove these people to produce and create, over and over. They didn't seem to be burdened with self-doubt and angst like himself; they roared forward, and when they got criticized they appeared genuinely shocked, as if the universe had somehow arrived upside-down and out of order. But no matter; those with "brass balls" would pick up right where they had last left off and move on, to the next project, unfazed.

It was early dusk, and Luka wanted to make good time this night, to reach the road crossing that finally forked away to Haslach. A half-day of rest had rejuvenated him, and the thought of the tracking party fading farther behind them made him eager to get started. He sat, enjoying a hard roll filled with salted ham, cheese and mustard.

Erik sat across from him, ogling his bit of painting yet again. His regular attention to it annoyed Luka. It was like watching an addict. "Would you put that away?" Luka finally bellowed.

Erik smiled and snickered, then turned to Luka, "You have your own 'little brown gypsy' now, yes?"

"What?"

"Your own painting, pulling at you, all the time. I see you, when you think I'm sleeping. I watch you staring at it, over and over."

Luka tossed the rest of his roll high onto the ridge and growled in frustration.

"It has a way of infecting you," Erik taunted, gazing at his own treasure again. "They're so amazing. Even if somehow they were just ordinary paintings; you know—that they didn't describe your life. They would still be mesmerizing. They're so...I don't know, alive in a way."

Luka opened his pack and began stowing items for the coming hike. "You talk too much."

Erik laughed. "Yes, I know. It used to drive Heisse crazy. That's why I started journaling. I needed someone to talk to, and Heisse wouldn't talk, just like you. So I started talking to myself through my journals. It turned out to be a great conversation." Erik laughed again.

Luka jumped suddenly to his feet and grabbed for Erik's pack. Erik's arm was partially through one strap. and the abrupt tug tumbled him sideways.

"AAAAAGH!" Erik shouted in pain. "What are you doing?" Erik lay splayed across the hillside.

"Are you writing now?" Luka shouted at him. "About you and me...this trip?"

Erik lay moaning on his side, trying to right himself with his good arm.

"Let me see! Give me your notebook, now!" Luka demanded, arm outstretched.

"Fuck you!" Erik managed as he pulled himself up. "So what if I am. It's not like I have to keep any secrets of yours now. SPY!"

"SHIT!" Luka shouted into the woods as he slammed his pack to the ground. He stormed down the hill.

"Stupid bastard!" Erik shouted after him.

Erik found Luka well after dusk, sitting at the bottom of the hill. He hobbled up slowly till he was standing beside him, but Luka wouldn't acknowledge.

"I know that look," Erik said. "That's the 'what the hell have I done?' look. I had that look a lot in the first days after I deserted."

Erik sat down with a groan.

"I have a mother and sister waiting for me in Frankfurt, waiting for the end of the war so that I can come home; but I can't go back there now. Maybe years from now after I hide out in Austria, after people forget about this war...then maybe I can go back to them...maybe. In the meantime my sister will hear that I was a deserter. My family will become outcasts for what I've done. And my mother, she's sick, how can I help her now? Sometimes when I think about it too long, I fall apart."

Luka still didn't answer or move.

"And now here you are," Erik continued. "You were a spy, deep inside Germany, far away from your home and loved ones. And now, you've left that all behind to follow a Nazi deserter back into the war, to find a warehouse full of magical paintings that can predict your future." Erik laughed.

Luka turned to look at him, with slow calculating intent. "If you're lying to me, I'll put a bullet in your head. I swear it."

Erik just laughed again. "Oh, I'm not lying. I promise you that." He stood slowly and flashed his own scrap of painting, turning it toward Luka so that he could see it again. "I don't know what we'll find when we get there." He turned the scrap back to himself and smiled at the drawing of the gypsy girl yet again. "Maybe the warehouse has already been emptied and moved by now. Maybe it's not near Haslach after all. Then you can go ahead and shoot me in the head, because you know what? At that point I won't care. I will have lost my family, my country, my future, and my little brown gypsy." He smiled at the treasure one last time, then put it back in his pocket and looked up at Luka. "Believe me, I want to get back there as badly as you do. Worse."

Luka studied Erik. He hadn't considered all that Erik had risked and given up to be here now, traveling alongside him. Erik smiled at him in response and held Luka's pack out to him. "Come on, let's go."

Luka took his hand, pulled himself up, and off they went into the night.

Chapter 26

The summer before his sophomore year, Luka was offered a deal similar to that of his freshman year. Work as a foreman, this time leading a summer construction crew on campus, for more money and room and board, with unfettered access to the arts lab. As May turned to June, Luka looked forward with hope to getting back to the nirvana of the previous summer, to rediscover the wonder of his craft.

It wasn't to be, though. The nagging doubts of the year pursued him into the summer and now into the clay. There were still random days of ecstasy, letting go in the moment, being lost in the inspiration. But the majority of that summer, "brass balls" eluded him. The art had become work, effort; it had grown difficult and uninspired, and Luka was lost.

They made steady progress in the early night following the dirt road to the east. Artillery and grenade explosions continually lit the night sky to the northwest. After midnight, convoys of German reinforcements came up the road from the south, and they had to move back to tree line to stay out of sight. The ground was uneven, the going slower, and soon Erik was limping noticeably; Luka caught him wincing in pain more than once. Finally, with a sigh of resignation Luka turned and led them up and away from the valley, over a low hill. On the far side they were sheltered inside a small false saddle, just out of view of either valley, so Luka lit a small fire. He dug in his knapsack for a few tins of fruit, but as he turned to offer one to Erik he found the man already fast asleep.

Luka climbed the higher west ridge and found what he was hoping for: he was atop one of the higher points for several kilometers around. He finally had a clear view in multiple directions, and the flashes from the shelling let him see details far to the north and west. They were exactly where he had expected they were, a little over five kilometers south of Haslach. He had anticipated seeing the glow of the town in the distance, but the shelling had probably scattered the inhabitants and there were only scattered points of light ahead.

The clear view also revealed a swarm of trouble that lay ahead. Luka could see traffic on every road heading north; troops, artillery, supplies, even on the small dirt road to the east he had hoped to find empty. They were indeed headed right into the junction of the fighting. Jack's information, as always, was exact; the war was coming to Haslach with a vengeance. Within a week this entire valley would be overrun with Allies advancing from the west. Luka sighed and laid down under a small pine to catch a quick nap.

Back at camp Luka watched Erik sleeping restlessly, tossing and turning against the chill of the night. The first purple hues of dawn were just creeping up the eastern horizon.

Suddenly Erik yelled long and loud, "AAAHHH!," and sat up erect and awake. For a few moments he peered nervously into the night, groping for recognition; and then the realization of where he was came over him and he slowly relaxed. He rubbed his leg and grimaced in pain.

"Bad dreams?" Luka asked.

"I was back in the foxhole with Heisse, after we were hit. There was his body torn in half, and me screaming for help. But no one came."

After a long pause Erik continued, "That whole day, there was screaming all around us on the hillside, just like mine. The shelling was right on top of us. I lost so many comrades."

Luka began tying down the packs, searching for something to say in acknowledgement, but could find nothing.

"I would like to hike a bit this morning," he finally stated, "along this small valley we're in. There's no trail, but it's flat, and we can follow it north in-between the ridge lines for a few more kilometers, travel slowly, away from the roads. We're close to Haslach now, but we need to get there. The front is closing in around us."

Erik nodded. "Yes, sure." Then after a few minutes he circled the conversation back. "Is that one of the things you did? As a spy...discover German troop positions, report back where we were, so that we could be shelled?"

Luka continued tying the packs down, not answering.

"You seem to know exactly what to do out here. You've trained, done this before, yes?"

Luka stopped and turned to face Erik, a tin of peaches in his hand. Erik wasn't going to let this discussion go. "Yes, that's part of what I did." Luka studied Erik but could discern no reaction. "And yes, because of my reports, sometimes German military positions were shelled."

Erik stared at the ground. "Does that make you angry?" Luka asked, "Does that make you want to kill me, here, right now?" Luka reached the can of peaches out across the little campfire. Erik looked up, then took the can.

Erik answered with his own question. "Is that why you don't sleep around me?"

Luka raised his eyebrows in surprise, then sat back against a rock, and began digging in his pack again. "Yes," he answered honestly, and added "no offense, it's just precautionary. Part of my training."

Erik ate slowly. "No, it doesn't make mad. You did your job...so did I. You were there to stop the Nazis. I was there to rebuild the Fatherland for all Germans." He paused and added, "But I can't tell you now what we were fighting for that day in the foxhole when I almost died with Heisse."

A long silence passed between them, then Erik added, "I mean...that day, we were there to stop those tanks from entering the valley. I know that. But the battle before that, I can't remember what the objective was." Erik paused again, staring into his tin of peaches. "And I'll bet if I'd stayed and lived, then the next week when I was fighting with Heisse in some new foxhole, I wouldn't be able to tell you why we were there the week before."

Erik threw his can down in disgust, and peaches spilled out across the rocks. Luka ate his own in silence as Erik continued staring at the ground.

Chapter 27

His junior year, something snapped deep within Luka's spirit. The struggle to be a degreed artist was too great, too stressful, and he began to convince himself that being an artist was no longer something worth pursuing.

Even though he was horrible at math, Luka knew the statistics quite well; that most of the graduates with fine arts degrees didn't make money right away, for many it took years. Several of Pennington's past graduates went on to work in factories, blowing glass for discount chains at a station, factory glass making just one stage in a larger series of steps—over and over and over again. He personally had a friend that spent the summer apprenticing at a pottery factory where he "put the handle on the mug", as his friend described it. The true artists, the ones all the freshmen admired and discussed at length, were already out there. They had ignored college and were creating pieces; they were living on ketchup and parmesan cheese but producing art, waiting to be discovered.

To Luka it boiled down to three choices: you taught, became a museum curator or an art expert for some local newspaper, or you became one of the exceedingly rare "true artists."

The logic seemed true enough, but the analysis lacked heart, and passion, it was missing that quality that "brass balls" cherished most. Luka just wasn't sure whose logic it was; his own, or his father's. He couldn't decide if his father would have been proud of him or not for his new knowledge. But the more he wondered about it, the less he wanted to know the answer.

Erik awoke, surprised to find himself alone in the darkness before moonrise. Sweeping his eyes along the top of the ridges, he spied Luka monitoring the south intently with his binoculars. Erik rose slowly. He was stiff all the time now—stiff when he walked, stiff after he slept; it seemed there was no escaping the pain in his leg.

He slowly hobbled up to the hilltop, trying to stretch his leg out. Luka lowered his field glasses momentarily to acknowledge Erik's approach, and then went back to intently watching the south again, the way they had come.

"Aren't we heading out?" Erik asked quietly.

Luka kept the binoculars raised to his eyes and responded, "not yet."

"You're looking south? We're supposed to be headed north, aren't we?"

Luka lowered the glasses, offering them to Erik. "Yes. Ettenheim is being shelled, a night bombing raid."

Erik looked, and although they were too far north and into the hills to make out the details of the town nestled in the valley, Erik could clearly see the orange glow of fire painted across the horizon. Every so often a yellow-white flash would rise brighter, followed by a low boom of thunder.

"I don't hear the bombers," Erik stated.

"You won't, they're way too high up. They bomb from tens of thousands of feet, to stay out of range of the anti-aircraft guns."

"Jesus," Erik whispered at another massive flash of white rising up. "Why Ettenheim?" he asked.

Luka didn't answer directly. "Well," he paused. "I'm not exactly sure, but I think the Allied campaign has moved away from bombing just war manufacturing. I think it's moved to terrorizing the public now."

"What?" Erik lowered the glasses, to see Luka's face.

"Break down support for Hitler. Break the German spirit, make sure the country knows the war is unwinnable. Maybe even incite an assassination attempt?"

"You don't think they already know that?"

"The people know it, they whisper it. But they won't come out and say it, not in public. It's the elephant in every German living room."

Erik stared back at Luka in disbelief.

"I'm sorry," Luka muttered.

"What? You're sorry?" Erik repeated, incredulously.

Luka didn't answer. He knew the apology sounded empty and hollow in the wake of the destruction taking place in front of them. Luka stood and walked to the far side of the ridge, emotion welling up within him.

"You're sorry for what? Did you call in the airstrike on Ettenheim yourself? Is that what you're sorry for?"

Luka turned to speak, and Erik saw there were tears in his eyes. "When I first got here, moved to Trier, I would find myself multiple times a day going over my cover story—repeating it to myself, to make sure I knew it. I was terrified I would be discovered, that I couldn't pull it off. But as the weeks turned into months, and then years, I found myself loving Trier, loving the people, loving this part of Germany. I went to local parties, to the pub, the festivals in the summer—I was just one of the townsfolk. There were neighbors that were wary of me, the 'smuggler'; I wasn't to be trusted. But there was a handful of people I grew to be good friends with. We were all just doing what we needed to, to get by."

Luka paused, gazing off into the darkness, gathering his thoughts. "My job spying grew to be something completely separate from my life as an art dealer and smuggler in Trier. As if the German

Army was somehow disconnected from the German people. I would go out on recon, spy on troop movements, recommend air strikes and artillery positions; but then I would go back home to my little village."

Erik looked at Luka, confused.

"I was spying on soldiers, the Nazis. Not Germans, you know, people like you, or Claudia, or my other friends. Those were the people I went back home to, my life. Somehow I never really linked what I was doing to the people around me. It was just...something that was necessary. What I was sent to do. And I was good at it."

Luka paused again, trying to collect himself. "No, I didn't call in this particular airstrike on Ettenheim tonight, but I might as well have. I've recommended dozens just like it."

Erik softened, watching Luka grasp in the darkness for something that would help explain the destruction they witnessed from a distance.

"I never put together that the war would eventually be over, and I would have to move on. I actually wondered if I might be able to live here afterwards."

Luka tucked his knees into his armpits.

"I loved this place," he finished. "And now it's gone for me."

Chapter 28

The small valley stayed tucked in between two parallel ridges running north until it emptied at an east-west road crossing. Luka and Erik stayed hidden in the trees, watching. German ambulances crossed intermittently, carrying wounded; from the northwest the shelling and explosions were louder now. They were still behind the German side of the front, but not far from it. At one time that had seemed reassuring to Luka, but now no side of the war was safe for him.

They waited until nightfall to cross the road and climb up the opposite hillside continuing north. The hills were gentle and rolling, but now even the smallest rocks and stones sent Erik flailing for balance, and their progress grew slower and slower. At the top of a hill they stopped to take a break. Erik was grimacing, in noticeable pain, rubbing his left leg.

"Erik," Luka started, "Why don't you stay here while I go..."

"NO!" Erik shouted back.

"I know you want to get to the warehouse. I'm just saying, I could scout ahead, find it quickly, and come back and get you. If I'm right we still have a few kilometers to go. I could get there and be back before…"

"NO!" Erik repeated. "I'm going with you." He stood up and resumed his hobbling gait into the darkness.

"Erik," Luka called to his back. "You're not going to make it."

But Erik wasn't listening. Luka sighed, picked up his pack, and followed.

Near daybreak Erik gave in and collapsed in the shade of a tall evergreen. Luka went on ahead to the top of the next rise and saw Haslach clearly in the distance, maybe three kilometers away. With his binoculars he scanned to the south of the village. The end of a gray cinder-block building was just visible, but the remainder lay hidden by the hills. Could that be the warehouse?

Luka went back to find that Erik had unloaded his pack and set out bread, cheese, and two tins of ham. His stomach rumbled in reply, grateful for some food and rest. They ate in silence, and Luka noted that more than once Erik rubbed his sore shoulder, grimacing in pain.

"Erik," Luka started, "I'm sorry for grabbing you back there, yanking you to the ground. That was stupid of me."

"Oh…I know," and then after a pause Erik added, "And if it helps, the only journaling I've done since Trier was my night out on the chalk ledge. I haven't mentioned you at all."

"Thanks," Luka answered.

"Are you American?" Erik asked.

"Yes."

"Your German is flawless."

"I know. My grandparents are first generation, originally from this part of Germany, so I already knew the area. They own a German deli in a little town outside Minneapolis, in the northern U.S. These fat Hausfraus and Omas come from miles around in the mornings to buy wurst, pickled eggs, kraut, weiss beer... I worked there every summer as far back as I can remember, heard and spoke German all day long. Sometimes I would work a Saturday and not speak a word of English the whole day."

"Really?"

"Oh yeah, that place helped pay my way through college."

"Studying what?"

"Art. I started studying sculpture—clay mostly, some bronze castings, sometimes stone or marble. But then I switched. I have a degree in art history."

"Art history...now that's a surprise."

"Yeah...I was sure I would end up at the front pulling a trigger. But my best friend that I enlisted with, his father had connections. He got the two of us pulled out for Officer's School, and I tested high on the evaluation exam. They were ready to move me to officer's training, and then they discovered my family background, how well I knew German. One thing led to another..."

Erik shook his head and snickered, "A sculptor spy..."

"I know," Luka answered. "I miss it honestly, it's been a while. I used to really enjoy just shutting everything out, locking the doors, and getting lost in the clay. Sometimes I wouldn't even know what I was going to sculpt, I would just dig my hands in, forget everything else around me, focus on being in the moment, and it was almost as if I could find the sculpture hiding inside the clay, speaking back to me, asking to be freed."

Luka had been gazing away at the ground, lost in a memory. He looked up to find Erik intently watching him.

"And you?" Luka continued. "How did you get here?"

"Ah," Erik smiled. "Yes, well, let's see. I'm from Frankfurt-am-Main, far north of here. Have you been there?"

"No."

"Well, it's very different than here. Flatlands, lots of banking and finance mostly. My father owned a machine shop just on the outskirts; selling and repairing tractors and farm equipment. You turn right up the road in front of my house and you're headed into the city and the gasthoffs and museums; you turn left, and you're headed to the farms."

"I spent my summers working in my father's shop, but as I got older I started working the farms as a hired hand, in the fields cutting and stacking hay, or harvesting corn. My friends and I could get out of two weeks of school each fall bringing in crops. It was tough work, but great to be outside, away from studies. I volunteered every year, that's how I came to like farming."

"Sounds peaceful."

"It was all I knew at the time, but we struggled. Everyone did. There was a great depression after the First World War. It was very hard for a long time. There were lots of families with nowhere to work.

"But as I got older, things changed, as the Nazis came to power. My father, and all my friend's fathers, they were just struggling to build their businesses, take care of their farms, look after their families. My father used to talk to me about it, that we all needed to work together to rebuild Germany, to make her great again; that the Treaty of Versailles was a German humiliation and ruined our country. I thought that's what we were all working towards.

"Then Hitler was elected chancellor, and the government was dissolved shortly after. At first it seemed good; things got better. There were road building projects, people were able to work again. It seemed like we were back on the right path. Hitler said he wanted to unite all Germans across Europe under one great New Order, to rebuild

German pride from the disaster of the Weimar Republic.

"But then Kristallnacht came, the night all the Jewish businesses were destroyed. We started hearing more and more about Jewish treachery, and how they were holding the Aryans back; how they were getting rich controlling the economy, controlling us all, keeping good Germans from uniting together, from making an honest living, from rising back to a global power; that they were holding on to all the money."

Luka watched Erik's face against the growing dawn.

"But...some of the shopkeepers and bankers that my father worked with...they were Jews. I had known them all my life, grown up with them, we worked in the fields together as kids. Most of them had moved to Germany from Russia or Poland years earlier, Jewish immigrants pushed out by the Russian Communists; but until then we had all grown up side-by-side, everyone getting along, minding our own business. I never even thought of who went to church and who went to synagogue until then. Jewish bankers loaned the money to the farmers to plant crops every year. A Jewish financier had loaned my father the money to start his shop years ago. We used to go have dinner with his family once a year to pay off the loan and sign for another. We were friends..."

Erik shook his head in confusion.

"It was so hard to understand. Everything got stranger and stranger. My Aryan friends started openly mocking Jewish kids at school, beating, kicking, and spitting on them; saying horrible things. We had all known each other for years, but now it had all changed."

Erik was staring off, looking through the surrounding trees remembering a sad, lost memory. "And so did I." His voice trailed off.

"You started hating the Jews and communists if you wanted to stay a good German. The gypsies, the homosexuals, you started hating all of them, otherwise YOU would be questioned next. YOU must have something to hide too. You went along unless you wanted to be an outcast...So I went along."

Erik paused again.

"But we all loved Hitler, the youth. We thought he was saving Germany." Erik spoke with conviction, a speech well learned and repeated, but his face betrayed confusion and doubt. "Hitler was rebuilding Germany from all the evil out there that just wanted to keep us down after World War I. I went with a bunch of my friends to the Youth Rally in Nuremberg. It was massive—I'd never seen that many people together in one place. And when Hitler spoke it was like listening to the savior of Germany. He told us that we were the future, that he and our parents were building Germany just for us, the youth.

"Well...we all went down to the Arbitur academy the next day, before we were even out of secondary school, and joined the Nazi Youth Corps. It was a great honor. My mother and sister were so proud of me. We all got uniforms, knives; we learned how to salute, and to march." Erik scoffed at the memory, shaking his head.

"And then came the invasions, first Austria. Hitler had promised all along there would be no war. And the German soldiers were welcomed into Austria like conquering heroes without a shot ever being fired. Like the Austrians *wanted* to be reunited with the Germans.

"And then Czechoslovakia—right at the beginning France and Britain wanted to meet, and they talk with Hitler and say he can go ahead and divide up Czechoslovakia, so that the Germans could be united again. And Hitler signed the Munich Agreement right there, promising again that there would be no war.

"Everywhere he went, Hitler's visions were all coming true, rebuilding Germany, and the world seemed to approve, seemed to want to see a united Germany again.

"But then we invaded Poland..." Erik trailed off, his voice dropping away.

"And there I was graduating from academy, already signed up. I went the very next day to boot camp, it was just the next thing we were all supposed to do, you know? We all knew that's what came next. And we still trusted Hitler..."

Erik shook his head again and sat in silence.

"Do you miss your comrades?" Luka asked.

"Yes...terribly. They were my only friends for the last two years."

After a long pause Luka asked, "Do you regret deserting?"

"No...no, I don't," Erik answered directly. "I would have died out there that day, I'm sure of it. But I do feel like a coward for leaving my friends behind. They stayed, and probably died."

After a long pause Erik added absent-mindedly, "I wonder if they even know that I left?"

Luka let the question hang in the air. "Look...are you sure you don't want me to go on ahead while you rest? Just to scout the area and make sure it's safe. It's only about three klicks up the road; I would be back by nightfall."

"Thanks," Eric answered, "but I want to come."

"Look, you can trust me. It's just, if there are troops ahead, trouble...I'm just not sure you could make it out. If we had to escape."

"Yeah...that's true." Erik paused. "...but I'm coming with you."

Luka tried to think of something else to say but drew a blank. "Alright," he finally acquiesced. "Let's get some sleep, we'll be there tomorrow."

Chapter 29

Luka sat on the short milk crate on the porch of the old house, smoking a cigarette, his elbows propped on top of his knees. He'd earned his bachelor's degree just seven days before, and his bags and belongings stood packed on the porch of the old house on college row. His roommates had long since left, the parties over. There was a pall that hung in the late May air, and it wasn't just the continual strumming of impending war in Europe that intruded on every campus conversation now. It was the shroud that hung across his own future that had Luka chain smoking, waiting for Mark to arrive with the truck. The overwhelming question that dominated his thoughts were "what now?", and he could find no clear answer.

Five years, two grants, and one large loan later, armed with a bachelor's degree, Luka wasn't excited about any of his options. He could teach art history as a graduate student and go for his masters, and then his PhD, but why? PhD—piled high and deep—what would he do with more art history knowledge and a doctorate? The conflict in

Europe had made hiring tight, and he couldn't even find a curator's job, which up to a few years ago looked like a very comfortable position to land.

Mark's battered pickup rattled to the curb in front of the house. He had to lean into the horn to get Luka to move from his listless stare. "COME ON!" he yelled. "WE'RE GOING TO BE LATE!"

Luka stubbed his cigarette out on the porch and sluggishly gathered up a handful of boxes. "I'm still not even sure why we're doing this," he tossed out.

"Because I'm a patriot!" Mark shouted. "And because YOU don't have anywhere else to go. That's Why! NOW MOVE YOUR ASS!"

Luka tossed his boxes and bags in the back of the idling pickup. "I don't know about this. Pennington said I was a shoo-in for a graduate teaching slot. I could teach art history, or even German. I could start planning my post-doctorate; maybe I'm meant to teach."

He came around to the passenger-side window to find Mark slumped over the wheel with his eyes rolled back in his head, faking a snore. "UnnnnnnkkKHH!" he shot upright. "Boring shit, man, you already said so yourself.

"Look, we talked about this. I'm going to enlist, it's the right thing to do. But you do what you want. Just go and listen to the schpeel, OK? If you don't want to sign up, don't. You take the truck, come back here, and go renew your lease with Pin-head-ington. BUT RIGHT NOW YOU'RE

MAKING ME FREAKIN' LATE!" Mark laid on the horn again.

Luka couldn't help but crack up laughing. He opened the door and got in.

Luka woke just after noon. The heat was oppressive, and sleep was impossible for him. He mounted the hillside to observe and saw patrols to the west on foot, heading north as far as he could see, with convoys of troops moving in between them. The Germans were preparing for a large assault; he had seen formations like this before.

To the east there was little going on. Looking back the way they had come, the reinforcements had rejected the damp eastern valley for the paved western road. Every now and then he spied a footman, patrolling the eastern dirt road. With his binoculars he followed the eastern valley north, all the way to Haslach. It was practically empty. He could follow the ridge line, staying high and to the east, staying out of sight of the majority of the patrols, till just south of town, then cross over the hills for the last half-kilometer, and make it to the warehouse. He could recon the site, see if troops had made it that far yet, know what they were up against, scout a safe trail for Erik to follow, and still be back by nightfall. He grinned to himself. It would be good to be solo for a while, traveling fast and quiet.

Luka went back and checked on Erik, still fast asleep. He shouldered his pack and then was off, following the ridge, quietly and quickly.

The ridge wasn't as quiet as he had expected. More than once he had to lay flat and quiet in the undergrowth, waiting for a patrol to pass by and out of range in the valley below. But he still made good time and crossed over the last hill just before three o'clock; and there it was, a cinder-block warehouse surrounded by a fence, tucked away to the south of the village, out of sight.

Over the far ridge, even in full daylight he could see the flash of artillery fire, the Allied approach, but they were still at least five kilometers out. Around the warehouse, he saw no immediate threats. He found a grove of aspen that offered good shade, and settled in to watch.

After an hour of observing, Luka still had discovered no activity around the warehouse. No guards or patrols, no troops nearby. In fact, he couldn't even see a car, or any activity at all in or outside of the warehouse. It might already be empty, abandoned.

He reached into his pocket and found again the little swatch of painting. He badly wanted to head down and inside, check it out thoroughly on his own, but he also didn't want to risk Erik waking and then looking for him with so many patrols out. He replaced the painting in his pocket and turned to head back.

Coming over the last few rises, Luka could hear the commotion before he saw it. Slowly cresting a rise, he saw patrols dotting the opposite hillside where he had left Erik. Luka's heart leapt into his chest, but he kept his discipline and stayed quiet, dropping flat against the ground, then fishing out his binoculars slowly from his backpack behind, not taking his eyes off the hillside ahead.

He raised the lenses, bringing them into focus, wanting desperately to find Erik, safe and asleep. He didn't have to look far to find him. Three foot soldiers and two SS guards had Erik, standing, roped against the tall evergreen he had been napping under, chest pressed against the tree. It was the tracking party; they had persisted, and had finally caught up to Erik's slower pace. His shirt had been stripped away, and one of the guards was beating him across the back with a thick leather strap.

Luka slumped to the ground, unable to watch. He bit into one his knuckles to suppress a yell. Luka's mind raced, what to do, what to do... There were patrols on both sides of the ridge and in front of him, on foot, and in half-tracks, moving up and down both side valleys scouring the hillsides. He counted at least twenty men.

Luka could hear his heartbeat racing in his ears now. He was sick with confusion, unable to think of a way to help his companion. Luka raised the glasses back up to his eyes. The SS guard had stopped beating Erik and was now yelling at the back of his head. Erik's body shook and convulsed. Two of the patrolmen and the other SS guard had dumped his pack out on the ground and were rummaging through it, the contents scattered randomly. Blood was now pouring down his leg from the shrapnel wound.

Luka considered for a moment, could he shoot the officer? He had both his pistol and the rifle, but his target was at least one hundred meters away, making the pistol useless. And he hadn't taken the time to sight-in the soldier's rifle; he would have to trust it was accurate. He would likely hit the officer, but he doubted he could get a clean head shot and kill him. But he certainly couldn't kill all five, and a shot would just direct the patrols right to him. Luka lowered the binoculars again, trying hard to think.

And as he lowered the binoculars a patrol of five footmen came into view, just ahead, walking slowly up his own hillside, headed right towards his position, methodically probing and searching the brush as they went.

Luka's mind went into automatic. He stayed low in the undergrowth and backed slowly and smoothly the few feet over the crest of the hilltop. There was no way to clear behind him now, he would just have to hope his only danger lay ahead. Slowly, steadily he crawled down the slope until he could no longer see the patrol. He stopped momentarily to glance behind, and seeing nothing, got to his feet and ran, hard, down the small saddle between the two hills. As he ran he stayed just to the east and below the top of the ridge, the same direction he had just followed returning from the warehouse. Scanning east ahead and behind, there were no patrols that he could see. Luka ran hard until his lungs burned and his legs ached. In his mind he pictured the patrol approaching the hilltop, estimated how far away they were from it—how much time did he have, thirty seconds at most, no longer, they will reach the crest…just …now!

Luka spun around to face the direction he had just left, diving for the nearest scrub. His eyes stung from the sweat running off of his head, and his panting was kicking up dirt and twigs into his mouth and nose, but he didn't dare raise his head. He watched the hill in front of him intently.

Nothing…nothing…and then he spied the footman slowly top the summit, looking left and right, probing the brush beneath him. The soldier stood for a moment scanning in all directions, then turned and waved one hand in the air, and proceeded back the way he had come, back down the hill and out of sight.

Luka lay quietly, not moving, still catching his breath. Waiting until he was sure the patrolman had gone, when suddenly three shots rang out in quick succession—pistol shots. The echo rang through the valley and hung in the air for what seemed an eternity.

"No, no, no..." was all Luka could manage, whispering it over and over, and now his chest was heaving, on the verge of breaking down. "Oh God no...please no," he prayed, trying to keep his voice as quiet as possible, his eyes still glued to the crown of the hill in front of him.

Luka looked quickly around, then down into the valley to the east. He could see no one. He knew he should wait longer, for safety, but instead he rose, running back to the hilltop. He was still panting "no, no, no" as he cleared the hilltop, and brought the binoculars up to his eyes.

Erik had been shot through the head and back, at point-blank range. His body slumped, legs splayed out grotesquely, spread eagle around the trunk, the rope still hugging his chest tight against the tree, blood running out in a steady stream from the hole in his head.

Chapter 30

Luka had been on the hillside hiding in the aspen grove for over two hours now, well into dusk, and still he could find no sign of activity in or around the warehouse. The street lamps illuminating the front gate where the gravel lot met the road glistened under a steady drizzle. Luka shivered again, but made no effort to cover his soaked head against the growing cold.

As he lowered the field glasses he recalled again watching Erik tortured through them and heard the shots ring out, reverberating through his memory again. His chest began to heave and shudder. Realizing that he was about to cry again, Luka pressed his face into his arm to stifle any sounds until the wave of grief passed through him. The only person that he had confided in during the war was gone.

Sitting now soaked from the rain, under the aspen on the hillside, head sideways resting against his arm, Luka reached casually into his pocket and touched the scrap of painting again. Was it worth it, he wondered: all he had given up—his cover, his career, his citizenship; and now Erik, who had given his life. Was it worth it to finally be here?

"Hello?" a voice called out from the hillside next to him.

Luka jerked in shock at the unexpected sound, scrambling awkwardly behind the tree trunk.

"It's alright," it called out again. "Don't shoot." The voice was just loud enough for him to hear.

"Herr Meiter," it said, "I'm going to come out now"; and then cautiously, slowly, a short, stocky man walked from between the last row of trees on the opposite hillside, his hands partially raised. He gestured toward the warehouse, slowly lowered his arms, and began walking down the slope. "Come along please, this way," he directed, continuing to the fence.

Luka watched the man, not entirely sure what to do next.

"Quickly, if you please." The man was keeping his voice low, looking around nervously. "There have been troops crossing through the village the last few nights. It's important we get in and out of sight." The man paused and waited. Luka didn't move. "Please," he implored with a big sweeping gesture toward the warehouse. "I know you're there in the trees, Herr Meiter, won't you come in?"

Luka stood slowly and walked guardedly out of the trees and down to the fence surrounding the warehouse.

The man smiled to see Luka emerge. "This way," he waved, walking around the far corner of the fence and out of view.

Luka walked quickly down the slope, Luger ready, not knowing what to expect. As he rounded the corner he found the stocky man holding a gate open for him, watching all directions with caution. As he approached, the man smiled and gestured him inside.

"Quickly," he whispered.

Inside the gate, the man padlocked it behind them, then ushered Luka toward the front door of the warehouse.

They hurried quickly inside and the stout man shut the door behind them. "Ah...thank goodness. You made it safely." He spoke in the darkness, then lit a match and lifted it to a lantern. The wick caught, and a yellow glow grew from within, gradually illuminating the space.

They were inside a cinder-block apartment, rugs on the floor, sitting chairs and a couch against the walls. In the far corner stood a tall man in full Nazi Reich uniform, colonel's insignia on his collar, hands behind his back, smoking a pipe. He didn't make any gesture of acknowledgement, just stared at Luka.

The stout man unwrapped a scarf from around his neck, "Brrr! I don't care if it is summer, the evenings are brisk here in the hills," he cheerily announced. He reached out a chubby hand to Luka. "I'm Doctor Clauberg." Luka didn't take his hand but stood in silence, his eyes not leaving the colonel's. "And you are Luka Meiter, American spy," the doctor smiled and chuckled, then withdrew his hand. "You won't need that with us." The doctor pointed at Luka's gun. "We are happy you made it; we mean you no harm."

Something in the German officer's unwavering look told Luka this man was gravely dangerous.

"Ah...yes. I forgot," the stocky man started. "You lost the deserter this afternoon. It must still be a shock for you," he stated, matter-of-factly.

Luka turned to face him. "How did you know?"

The doctor just smiled, and then pointed. "Come...I'll show you."

Luka followed the doctor out of the apartment and into the cavernous space of the open warehouse. Ahead, mounted to the back of a large painter's easel, was a single lamp. Surrounding the easel, in the shadows, Luka could see rows and rows of paintings, standing one in front of another, all leaned against the walls, stretching out into the darkness to the end of the warehouse. The odor of fresh oils and turpentine hung heavy in the air.

"We don't dare light the warehouse at night any longer," the doctor spoke over his shoulder.

"Not with the troops so close. But we thought it necessary to leave this one out for you, just for tonight." The doctor stopped and gestured toward the canvas.

As Luka rounded the easel to face the painting, his jaw slowly dropped open. The canvas was nearly full, arcing from left to right, top to bottom, scene after scene flowing in beautiful detailed color, telling a sweeping story. Luka recognized Erik in bed asleep at the boardinghouse, Luka sitting beside him reading the journal by lantern; then the two of them hiding the car in the grove of scrub oak outside Ettenheim; running across the highway, with both packs in Luka's hands; Luka yanking Erik down by his pack strap on the hillside; sitting atop a ridge scanning the horizon, maps spread around his feet. And then...Erik strapped against the tree, the barrel of a pistol pressed against his head by the SS officer, the anger of the guards and the terror in Erik's eyes, and next Luka crouched in the rain on the hillside, watching the warehouse through his binoculars, hidden in the aspen grove.

Luka turned to face the doctor. "How?" was all he could manage.

The doctor smiled a big toothy grin. "Yes, amazing isn't it? That's how we knew you had arrived."

Part III – The Muse

Chapter 31

Luka sat at the artist's stool examining the painting in close detail. The brushwork and detail were exquisite, in no place were the paints over applied, and nowhere could he find a scene that had been painted over or otherwise corrected. The artist had a clear vision of each scene in his head before he started. There was no need for the artist to work as most did, by painting the background, and then the foreground over it, then more detail over that, continually covering at least part of the ongoing work; this artist knew at the outset what every point on the canvas was supposed to hold.

And he had never seen this level of composition before. The grain of sidewalks in one scene became the dark speckled shadows of trees in the next; the orange shading of the sun at dusk was just as accurately portrayed as the shadows cast at mid-day in the next scene. Nothing was interpreted; it was almost as if one were looking at a giant composite of photographs that had somehow been seamlessly blended, one into another, weaving a remarkable story.

Luka reached out and cautiously touched a small ridge of paint in the scene of Erik strapped to the tree. The oil skinned and gave way just slightly beneath his fingertip.

"You'll want to be very careful," a voice from the darkness spoke behind him. Luka turned to find the colonel standing in the shadows, watching him. "It's wet still, isn't it?"

Luka shook his head in disbelief, "Yes, it is."

"When are you moving us?" the Colonel asked, abruptly changing the subject.

Luka turned to face him. "Moving you?"

"Yes, that's why you're here, isn't it? We sent the deserter back to fetch you, to bring you the message to come and get us." The command in the colonel's voice was palpable. Even in conversation his sentences sounded more like orders.

Luka examined the colonel before responding. He stood erect, immovable, continuing to smoke his pipe, puffing and exhaling slowly and rhythmically. The colonel never took his eyes off of Luka, even as the doctor reentered the room.

"Yes, he delivered your message, and that is why I'm here." Luka answered. "But I'm not moving anyone or anything until I understand what's going on here." He gestured back to the painting. "How is this possible?"

"Yes, of course." The doctor interrupted cheerily. "And we expected as much." He walked forward with a tray filled with cups and a pot. He set the tray down on a table near the easel and began pouring a steaming cup of black coffee.

"Would you like anything in your coffee? Milk, honey?"

"No," Luka replied.

"Wise choice, because it's quite good on its own."

"I don't want any coffee," Luka clarified.

"No! Are you sure?" the doctor seemed genuinely hurt. "It's Viennese, just a hint of chocolate in it." He held out a cup toward Luka, trying to tempt him.

Luka didn't respond.

The doctor then turned to offer Luka's cup to the colonel, but he didn't budge either.

"Ahhf," the doctor scoffed. "What a waste of effort you both are. He turned back to the tray and began adding copious amounts of milk and sugar to his own cup.

"I want to know," Luka continued, his voice level and restrained, "how is it possible for you to paint our journey here, while we were still on the way? How did you know about the hilltop where Erik died, and then paint that exact scene in such detail?"

The doctor turned to the colonel. "We knew it would come to this." His tone was meant to restate the obvious.

The colonel turned and walked back into the apartment, measured and methodical.

The doctor turned back to Luka. "We knew where you would be, but we didn't know when...within a couple of days, anyway. Korzak just painted most of these last scenes this afternoon, of the deserter on the hilltop, and you waiting outside. I was just lucky you made it here this evening, otherwise I would have spent some long nights out there waiting for you to arrive." The doctor rolled himself off of the stool he was sitting on. "Follow me," he said.

Luka followed the doctor back into the apartment, then down a short hallway and into a smaller anteroom. The room smelled of decay, urine, and old age. It was barely lit by a small lantern.

The doctor leaned over and turned the lantern up so it illuminated the room.

In the brighter light Luka could now see an old, short man asleep in bed. He looked crumpled, mostly bald, with odd patches of red scaly skin, and wiry gray hair poking through in clumps along his scalp. The skin on his arms was veined, thin, and papery, but they lacked the purple blood scabs of old age. His eyes were closed, his mouth open, and a continuous line of mucous and drool ran onto the pillow. His breath came erratic and raspy, the sound of fluid rolling in his lungs just beneath his breathing.

"Luka Meiter, meet Breslaw Korzak. He's your miracle painter."

Chapter 32

"He's the artist?" whispered Luka.

"No need to whisper," the doctor stated matter-of-factly. "He's completely deaf, and mildly sedated. He was so agitated with your impending arrival. He gets that way when new people are near."

"He created the painting? The one I saw tonight?"

"Yes, all of them," the doctor answered merrily.

The doctor wiped Breslaw's mouth with a towel and straightened his head against the pillow. He lifted the sheets and looked underneath, examining the crumpled man up and down. "Years and years of practicing medical research, only to become a bedside nurse," he said in disgust.

He lowered the sheets and tucked them under the sleeping man. Breslaw snorted, turned slightly, then resumed his raspy breathing. "What I wouldn't give to have just one nurse here," the doctor muttered. "And we don't have the right medicine. Come, follow me. We should let him rest."

Back in the warehouse Luka flipped through stack after stack of paintings, trying his best to examine them by lantern. Outside in the darkness the drizzle had turned to rain, rattling noisily against the metal roof. And the war raged on; every now and then an artillery burst announced itself, large enough to light the skylights, like flashbulbs overhead, briefly revealing the massive quantity of paintings lining the walls. The doctor sat quietly beside Luka on a stool, sipping his coffee, letting him inspect the work.

Some paintings were happy wonders, glowing snapshots of bright lives well lived. This one started with an adoption, a dark-skinned boy being handed over to a young loving couple at an orphanage; later he's playing soccer, concentrating on a goal kick; then later still, bailing hay into a barn, the boy now a young man with the beginnings of a muscular physique, his entire life ahead of him.

Others started out bright and then changed into sullen broodings. This one told the story of a beautiful little brown-haired girl. First she was running and splashing through streams, chasing frogs, eyes wide with amazement and joy; the next singing in choir, her mouth opened in song; then as a teenager, carrying loaves of bread in a basket through a crowded slum, people pressed in around her; and then finally aboard a dirty gray train entering a dull, red-bricked archway, smokestacks belching white in the background.

Others were horrors from start to finish. Here an entire mass of people in gray-and-black stripes, climbing a bloody wall covered in barbed wire, mouths agape in silent screams. Behind them torturers with whips, guns, and chains, snarling dogs barely held on taut, long leads. A pile of dead laid open and eviscerated upon the ground, blood flowing in streams, as the mass attempted to climb up and over the dead.

"You know about the concentration camps?" the doctor asked Luka.

"I know some."

"Do you know any details?" the doctor asked.

Luka paused, "I've heard rumors, we all have. But most of the news I get is by courier. Everything else I heard through the townspeople, what the populace is told. I've never heard the rumors confirmed."

"Like what?"

"I heard that the Nazis are holding more than just prisoners of war. They're also relocating Jews, Slavs, homosexuals, migrants, the 'undesirables,'" Luka spoke it in disgust.

"But you know no other...details?"

Luka turned to look at the doctor. The continued questioning on these lines struck him as strange.

But the doctor quickly continued on without waiting for an answer. "The colonel was commandant at Gross-Rosen, inside Poland. A concentration camp built for the expansion east and on into Russia, and I was the chief medical officer. We started by housing prisoners of war, but quickly the camps began taking in others, non-Germans, non-Aryans. Mainly to repopulate the Polish countryside for the German New Order." The doctor stated this lightly,   as if narrating a newsreel.

"Korzak came to us almost two years ago now. At first he was slated for...work detail. But we quickly found out he was an artist of some repute in Poland. He became part of the colonel's personal staff, and was set to work for the officers—painting decorations on the walls of the officer's quarters; meeting rooms, things like that."

"And he could always paint like this?" Luka asked.

"The   quality...yes,   he   was   very accomplished..."

"No, I mean his prescience; was he always able to paint people's lives? See their past, and their future?" Luka clarified.

Just then, the colonel barged from the apartment into the warehouse. He was dripping rain from a long overcoat. "Troops are less than four   kilometers   north   of   the   city,   they're advancing. They will be here within four days, a week at the outside." He stomped to a halt directly beside Luka.

"I need to know how and when you're getting us out," the colonel barked.

Luka continued flipping through paintings, attempting to appear unperturbed by the outburst, but he could feel the beads of sweat prickling out on his forehead. The doctor sat in silence, staring into his coffee mug.

"Is it by American troops? Are we to be arrested? Will they carry us through the lines to France before they begin interrogating us, or through the west and into Russia?" the colonel waited for his answers. Luka dropped the stack of paintings he was looking at and turned to face the colonel.

"I already told you. Nothing is happening until I give the word."

The colonel started to speak, but Luka interrupted "You have a shortwave radio here?"

"Of course," the colonel blurted, clearly angered.

"I'm getting all of this, and you, out using smugglers, from my underground network." Luka answered back calmly. "Three trucks and men, one trip, all we can carry. In and out in one night, the rest stays behind. I set it up before I left using Erik's descriptions. These are men that I've worked with in the past to confiscate pilfered Nazi war treasures. They're loyal to me, and to my money. I trust them. They take a third of the paintings."

"Smugglers?" the doctor blurted. "No…that won't work!"

The colonel ignored the doctor and pressed on. "And why should I believe you?" he growled.

"Don't believe me!" Luka snapped back without hesitation. "Get it all out yourselves. Why haven't you already? Because you are running away at the head of the German retreat? Retreating from the Eastern front with your treasures in tow? You went AWOL and now you're wanted by the SS too."

The colonel continued staring, then dropped his voice even lower. "You really don't understand the gravity of this situation, boy. This isn't a game. If the Germans get here first, discover us from behind, then we're all captured and interrogated. They'll finally investigate your cover, discover who you really are, and we're all dead."

"But if the Russians get here first…" the colonel shook his head slowly from side-to-side. "They'll lock the four of us inside and burn this place to the ground without thinking twice about it."

"You're paranoid," Luka snapped back, trying to sound nonchalant.

"You Americans…" the colonel continued without missing a beat. "You don't really have a clue what's going on here in Europe, how long this war has really been brewing, the hatred. We thought we had decimated the Red Army, but then they pushed us back at Stalingrad. They're out for blood now. They want to be the first to Berlin, they want to beat you and the British there to skin Hitler alive; him and all of his commanders." He shook the colonel's bars on his collar at Luka.

"Korzak will never make it in the hands of smugglers!" the doctor squealed, sounding panicked.

Luka didn't reply.

"He's not well," the doctor continued, his voice high and thin. "Without constant care he will quickly slip away! We were expecting to surrender to you, the Americans. So we can get everything out at once!"

"It's the only way," Luka replied calmly. "I just have to give the word." He turned and went back to flipping through paintings.

"No!" the doctor whined.

"Ah," the colonel sighed. He threw his head back and chuckled, "I see now. You can't use American troops. You're here on your own!"

Luka dropped the stack of paintings again and stared back at the colonel. He could feel his own anger rising up in his flushed face, but he didn't dare back down now.

"Of course," the colonel laughed. "That's it. I should have realized as soon as you walked in. You're on your own."

"Alfred, this won't work!" the doctor's tone continued to rise.

"I've already told you how we're getting out. I'm not giving any orders until I get the whole story here." Luka turned back to the stack of paintings. In his anger he wasn't even aware of what he was looking at any longer. He half expected the colonel to pistol-whip him across the back of his neck.

The colonel turned to leave, still laughing. "Don't worry, boy. You'll get the rest of your story. More than you could possibly want to know."

"Alfred!" the doctor shot out of his chair and ran behind, protesting to the colonel's back.

As they walked back into the apartment Luka could hear their conversation fading.

"Alfred, you know how sick he is! This isn't what we talked about."

"Stop sniveling, this could work out even better. We get to wait the rest of the war out, just in a new place, that's all," the colonel snarled.

"But it's smugglers, Alfred! There's no telling where we'll end up. If I don't have access to a medical clinic, he'll die!"

"THEN YOU'LL JUST START OVER, WON'T YOU?" the Colonel blared. A door slammed, and any remaining discussion was lost to Luka as muffled shouting.

Chapter 33

Luka lay in his little bed in the warehouse staring at the ceiling. The muffled arguing between the colonel and the doctor had ceased over an hour ago. The doctor had come cheerily back into the warehouse to show Luka to his room for the night, giving away no hint that there had even been an argument, and Luka didn't inquire further. But lying in bed, he had the nagging, uneasy feeling that falling asleep here could be a disastrous mistake.

Once during the night he had heard loud snoring through the wall behind the head of his bed, and decided it must be the painter. He tried to envision the broken old man he had seen earlier painting all of those pictures, but every time he tried to imagine it, he could only shake his head in disbelief.

Luka swung his legs over the side of the bed and sat up. The deep darkness of the apartment with no windows was eerie and unnatural, like the black ink of a cave. The lack of dimension from even the faintest light was disorienting. Outside, the rumble of the war continued, unabated; the night and ongoing rain did little to suppress it. The front did indeed sound closer now. He could make out the smaller explosions of RPGs and grenades in between mortar rounds. But deep inside the closed-off warehouse it was impossible to see the flashes of artillery and thus judge distance.

Sighing, he realized he wouldn't be getting any sleep tonight.

Luka took his Luger, cycled the action to make sure there was a shell in the chamber, snapped the safety on, and then stuffed it down the back of his pants. He dressed, leaving his boots, and went carefully out into the dark hallway, where he stood and listened. It was hard to concentrate on the sounds of the open warehouse over the constant thunder of shelling in the distance, but after several minutes of waiting, he decided there was no one else awake.

Slowly and gingerly he walked through the dark hallway, his left arm out, gently brushing the wall. Try as he might his eyes couldn't adjust, and trying to probe visually only left him straining. His head was throbbing as he tried to concentrate to see anything in the thick darkness. His footsteps landed softly on the rugs covering the concrete floor, but his breathing was shallow and rapid, so he stopped again to calm himself.

Stop, reach the corner. OK, turn; now the long hallway. Farther on to the left is the opening to the warehouse; beyond that is the kitchen to the right, the front entrance, and the other apartments. Better to explore the warehouse first, look there for an exit. Try to map where Erik first entered, what direction his hiding place had been. That makes two exits out of the warehouse that you know about; there could be more. Careful, slowly, feel the wall, calm down, breathe easier, deeper breaths.

Ahead a faint light came into view, framing the open doorway leading into the warehouse. Luka reached it, backed against the far wall, and slowly and silently moved to see out into the warehouse. To the far left he could see the light clamped onto the back of the artist's workstation had been left on. Otherwise the warehouse was dark. He listened for a moment longer, heard nothing else, and walked into the vast open space.

"Looking for something?" came rolling deep and low from the darkness.

Luka visibly jumped, nearly stumbling to the floor. He turned to see the colonel standing on the far side of the warehouse, quietly smoking his pipe in the darkness. Luka tried to put a brave face on his shock. "Shit, you scared me."

"Then don't go sneaking around my warehouse at night," the voice came back, low and silky smooth.

"I can't sleep...can't get these paintings out of my head," Luka lied.

There was no answer for a moment. Then Luka saw the quick yellow burst of a match flame, and the glowing red bowl of a pipe being drawn upon. Luka felt a surge of reminiscence for Jack, and the barn.

The colonel finally chuckled low, "Yes, they do have that effect, don't they?" He walked just out of the shadows and into the light, still in full Nazi officer's dress. The crispness and formality of the uniform were unnerving, it automatically set Luka on edge. He decided the effect was designed to do exactly that.

"I've been looking for a particular painting," the colonel said, "one that I'm sure you would like to see." He turned and began flipping paintings forward, briefly examining one, then moving to the next. "It's here near the front, somewhere close to the easel, I know that."

He turned to face Luka and gestured, "Come over here, help me look."

Luka moved cautiously toward the colonel. "What am I looking for?" he asked tentatively.

"Oh, don't worry. You'll know it when you see it. Believe me," the colonel answered. "It was finished just a couple of days ago...it's close by."

Luka walked cautiously to the colonel's side and leaned the first painting in a stack out before him. His heart was pounding, but he forced himself to view the paintings he was handling. A family, possibly triplets, visiting a beach, a hospital stay...next, a young couple in bed, making love; a baby arriving; then another baby...next, an athlete, a gymnast, family and friends cheering her on at a meet; then a truck and men with guns surrounding her and her family; then she's in a railroad car; next she's screaming in terror, struggling in the mud, as her mother and father are dragged away from her.

"We just aren't very organized here," the colonel mumbled. "It's here in one of these two stacks, I'm sure."

The next picture Luka flipped up didn't look at all like the others. Surrounding the painting on all sides were people; hundreds of them, piled one on top of the other, all dressed in drab gray with black stripes, crying and screaming, howling, clawing; some bleeding terribly, directing all kinds of anger, fear, hate, and terror toward the much larger man in the center. And then Luka realized the man in the center was the colonel. It was a striking portrait of the man, from his shoulders on up, in full uniform.

Luka glanced at the colonel standing in profile. The resemblance was remarkable. In the portrait he was looking off in the distance, focusing on something far away, not in the painting; but Luka recognized completely the attitude captured on his face—of cruelty, surety, dominance, arrogance. Luka could hardly breathe.

"I think I found it..." Luka managed.

The colonel reached over to pull it up in the light shining from the easel. "Ah, yes. I remember this. Well, it's not the one I'm looking for, but it IS quite remarkable, don't you think?"

The colonel turned to look at him, but Luka didn't respond.

"It's from the concentration camp at Gross-Rosen, one of the ones Korzak painted just before we left to come here. I probably would have shot the little bastard for painting it at another time, eh?" and he chuckled out loud.

Luka stood stunned, in silence.

The colonel smacked him across the arm. "Oh, come now. Get a hold of yourself. This isn't real!" the colonel chuckled again. "You see, our little painter not only can paint your life's story; he has a nasty streak in him as well. He's been around either the doctor or myself every day for months now." The colonel dropped the painting and went back to thumbing through his stack. "That's simply his way of getting back at me."

"For what?" Luka managed.

But the colonel answered with, "Ah...here it is." He pulled a large partially finished painting out with the greatest care and walked over to the easel. "Come and see it in the light, you'll love this," the colonel beckoned, and he placed the painting in the center of the large easel.

Luka walked to the easel. The painting was of him, Luka, his life. In the upper left corner his mother was dressed in a coat, holding him as a baby, rocking him to sleep, wrapped in a thick wool blanket, her eyes nearly shut from exhaustion, patting his back gently, her breath drawing two thin streaks of steam in the night air. Luka remembered hearing the story—the big black enameled rocker, being sick with croup, his mother opening all the windows on the front porch in the dead of a Minnesota winter so that he could breathe easier.

Next he was a boy, lying on his stomach on the floor, drawing, kicking his legs. Little white socks with red bands and the black oval soles of his shoes waving happily in the air; papers, markers, and crayons spread in every direction surrounding him; through a far doorway his father was opening the door for his uncle, who was standing in tears on the doorstep. Luka felt a sudden pang of remembering—the day he found out his aunt had died of Lupus, the day before Thanksgiving. How the house had gone from the warmth and happiness of the holiday, to adults hiding in doorways, hugging and weeping; until he came in the room, that is, and they would smile back at him through red-rimmed eyes, pretending as if everything were somehow going to be the same.

Then he was standing on a baseball diamond at home plate, bat at his feet, umpire and catcher standing, surrounding him, clutching his mouth, blood dripping from between his fingers. Luka remembered—trying out for baseball. To practice, he and his dad would hit balls in the backyard, and Luka could consistently hit home runs three yards away. Going to tryouts, and getting beaned by the opposing pitcher, a fastball squarely to the mouth. Ten stitches later, Luka wouldn't go near a baseball bat, and that was the end of his, and his father's, hopes.

Next he was a teenager, sitting at an artist's stand, a mound of clay in front of him. One hand buried deep within, the other steadying the wet ruddy-brown mass against his probing. A sly smile across his face, and Luka remembered the sweet surety of those days; of being exactly where he wanted to be, doing exactly what he wanted to be doing.

Luka looked slowly back at the colonel in stunned silence, tears welling up in his eyes.

"Yes," the colonel responded, "I know. They can be like that. Stunning and sensual."

He paused for a moment. "Before you judge us all too harshly here, consider the miracle you're discovering. What's really being created here."

The colonel paused again, and then smiled a most disarming smile. "You can have a piece of that for yourself." And then another pause. "Good night, Luka. Stay out here as long as you like."

The colonel walked back into the apartment and left Luka alone, with the beautiful treasure of his life recorded before him.

Chapter 34

Luka woke to the low rumble of thunder, loud and close, vibrating through his body. He opened his eyes to find he was lying on the concrete floor of the warehouse, the glow of morning hue trying to break through the dingy skylights above him. He had fallen asleep at the base of the easel, below his painting.

He sat up slowly to a cramped and twisted neck, when another deep rumble shook the floor, rattling the skylights and sending the bottles on the work area tinkling against each other. It wasn't thunder, it was artillery shelling, and it was close.

Luka stood rubbing his sore neck and shoulders as the doctor entered the warehouse. "Ah, there you are," he said upon seeing Luka. "Oh no, did you fall asleep out here?"

Luka nodded slowly, still rubbing the crick from his tender neck.

"I'm so sorry. Are you hungry?"

"Yes," Luka managed.

"Good!" the doctor seemed genuinely pleased. "I've made breakfast for us. Come." He led the way into the kitchen. Food was everywhere;

the doctor had been busy. Boiled eggs, slices of cooked ham and bacon, Danish pastries, toast, butter and jam, a big steaming pot of jet-black coffee at the center of the table. Luka's stomach rumbled in response, and he began filling a plate.

"The colonel gets up very early, before me. And it's such a waste to make a full breakfast just for me," the doctor rambled.

"Will the colonel be joining us?" Luka inquired.

"Oh no, he's already gone. Lately he spends the mornings watching the troop movements around us. He's very concerned we'll be overrun."

As if in response, another rumble shook the building.

"And it seems he's right..." the doctor added. He's seldom wrong, the colonel."

Across the room Luka noticed another stack of paintings in the hallway, against the kitchen door frame. Luka leaned back to get a better look.

He turned to see the doctor watching him, chewing on a big piece of ham. "Please," the doctor gestured with his knife toward the stack of paintings.

Luka stood, carefully wiping his hands, and proceeded into the hallway. He retrieved the stack, sat down again at the table, and examined the first painting in his hands. It was the same pattern, scene after scene from someone's life, one corner of the canvas flowing out and around telling the life of the person. Most of the scenes were of a woman in a nurse's uniform.

"Ah, I remember that one," the doctor managed through a mouthful of toast.

"One of the nurses that worked for me at Gross-Rosen."

Luka looked up at the doctor. He was leaning back in his chair, lost in thought.

"An excellent nurse. But she took off after Korzak finished that painting," the doctor chuckled. "Just up and left one day, never returned to work. I don't know what became of her."

Luka turned back to the painting. Just off center to the upper right was a scene of two women in bed, holding each other tenderly, making love.

"She was a lesbian, and no one knew it till then. Until Korzak exposed her." The doctor laughed a guttural laugh.

Luka turned back to stare at him.

"Oh, mind you. I don't care. Not at all, but that sort of thing is frowned upon in the Nazi party. No homosexuals!" the doctor wagged his finger in mocking rebuke.

"You're sure this is accurate, that she really was a lesbian?" Luka asked.

"Yes. By the time he had painted this one, we knew what he was capable of, that he could see into people's pasts. He was doing it on a daily basis. All of the people that surrounded him in the infirmary; me, the nurses, the other doctors, prisoners, guards, the colonel. Anyone that came near him."

Luka continued staring at the painting. It was sweeping and beautiful, the nurse holding the hands of children gazing up at her in more than a few scenes.

The doctor had finished eating and was lighting a cigarette to go with his cup of coffee. Now he was leaning back, searching the ceiling for memories.

"He seems to focus on the more defining moments of a persons' life. Even if they don't realize the moment is important to them. You should see the ones he's done of me and the colonel." The doctor clucked and shook his head.

"He's done paintings of the two of you?"

"Oh, yes! Many, many paintings of us. We've been the only people around him for the last several months, at least close around him. I'm afraid he's grown very, very sick of us by now." Then the doctor added somewhat lower, "and us of him."

"This is remarkable," Luka whispered at the canvas, "but I don't see how..."

"RIGHT!" the doctor slapped both of his hands down hard on the table. "Let's go get him up, shall we? You need to understand."

Chapter 35

Luka followed the doctor into Breslaw's room. The old man was awake already, still under the covers, his eyes darting back and forth across the ceiling, appearing to focus on nothing in particular.

"Alright, come, Korzak," the doctor started. "Yes, yes, soooo exciting." Breslaw's head was now rolling back and forth. "Oh, I know, we have a visitor, don't we!" he cooed like he was talking to a child.

The doctor yanked the sheets back, then turned and fumbled in the nearby dresser for a change of clothes.

Luka stared at the frail man lying before him. His legs were bare, thin sticks, colored a peculiar purple-ashen hue that didn't match the rest of his skin tone. His feet were almost stumps, grossly misshapen with curled-under toes. They didn't look as if they could come close to supporting his body weight.

The doctor had turned back to the bed and was roughly pulling the little man toward him legs first. Luka winced at the severity of it, and reached from the other side of the bed to help.

"NO!" the doctor shouted suddenly, 'DON'T TOUCH HIM!" The outburst made Luka jump. "Please..." the doctor repeated, more calmly, "please only let me touch him." He grinned an awkward little apology of a smile. "There's a reason I ask this, which you'll soon discover."

Luka watched the doctor work through the morning ritual. He stripped Breslaw naked, revealing an adult diaper that he proceeded to change. The smell of concentrated urine and feces filled the room.

"I don't understand," Luka said. "From what I see here, you never would have taken a man in his condition into the concentration camps. A bedridden elderly man who can't even function on his own."

"Yes, well...that's true enough," the doctor agreed. He was deftly running a clear tube into Breslaw's nose and down into his chest. The sudden intrusion made Breslaw jerk in reflex, and he began coughing a deep, rolling cough of thick phlegm. The doctor alternately pulled and pushed the tube in and out of Breslaw's chest, suctioning out the congestion as he coughed.

"Then how..." Luka started.

"He became...disabled, in camp," the colonel confirmed from behind. He was standing ominously in the doorway, dressed in a heavy overcoat. "Doctor, we talked about this," he continued. "We're out of time. You tell him what he needs to know, so that we can get out of here. He needs to decide he's a part of this," the Colonel ordered. "I'll be outside." With that, he stormed out of the doorway.

The doctor shook his head slowly in resignation and pulled Breslaw up to the edge of the bed, legs hanging over the side. "I wouldn't be surprised if he leaves us all here, the colonel," he muttered. He was now dressing Breslaw, manipulating his thin red arms into a cotton shirt. Luka briefly glimpsed a blue numbered tattoo on one arm as it was pulled inside the sleeve. Then the doctor was buttoning the shirt, bent forward, gut creased, fumbling to find the button holes across the little shell of the old man.

"Take the car and just leave," the doctor continued. He had finished dressing Breslaw, and had turned to a small dressing table in the room. "Probably shoot us all before he goes, though." He was now mixing dry paste and water into a bowl, stirring it with a spoon.

Breslaw sat on the edge of the bed, his head still rolling around, neck back, then forward; looking at nothing in particular, although Luka could see no visible signs of blindness like a cataract. The old man's pupils seemed clear and bright; but although he looked around, he never seemed to focus on anything in the room, including Luka or the doctor.

"Is he blind?" Luka asked.

The doctor had turned back to face Breslaw, a bowl of oatmeal in his hand. "Mmmm" he cooed, "time for our morning mush, eh?" and he began feeding Breslaw. The doctor had to wipe his mouth in between servings; Breslaw chewed and swallowed, the entire time his head rolling oddly around, forcing the doctor to chase his mouth with the spoon.

"Yes and no. Technically he should be able to see, but he's had a mental break. His eyes function normally, but he chooses not to focus on the outside world any longer. Only when he wants to," the doctor answered.

"But he knows we're here?"

"Oh, yes, very definitely." Breslaw's head rolled back and forth, side to side, as if his muscles couldn't hold it upright on the thin frame. "You don't know him, but this is a lot of excitement he's showing right now, ISN'T IT, KORZAK!" he shouted, lowering his face to his ward. Breslaw didn't react, but continued chewing and rocking his head back and forth. The doctor chuckled, "but he's completely deaf."

"How old is he?"

"Hmmm," the doctor looked away in thought, "let me think." He was wiping the little man's mouth, turning back to the dressing table again. "I figured it out once...from his records," the doctor continued. He turned back to face Breslaw, syringe now in hand, full of a silver-tinged, milky-white substance. The doctor began fumbling inside

Breslaw's shirt. "You know," he said to Breslaw, "you and I are going to have to put in a new stint one of these days soon. We've been putting it off, but we're not going to make it much longer with this old one."

"How old?" Luka reminded him.

The doctor had found the chest tube and was injecting the mixture slowly into Breslaw. "Oh yes," he remembered. The doctor had finished, and was now facing Luka, empty syringe sticking up in the air in mock salutation. "Forty-seven," he announced confidently.

Chapter 36

The doctor pushed Breslaw into the warehouse and toward the workstation. He was seated in a rolling high-backed chair that was extended precariously high to the end of its screw length. Breslaw sat pressed against the back with a long makeshift waist belt wrapped around his chest and over his waist so as not to fall over. The seat and back were padded with worn, gray, stained foam rubber. It looked as though he had passed many a day in that old padded chair.

Luka hadn't responded to the doctor's last answer. In disbelief, Luka was growing more angry at the doctor's evasiveness. "I want to know why," Luka grumbled.

"Yes," the doctor answered, resigned. "I know. We owe you answers," he acknowledged. "You're just not going to want to hear them all at once."

The doctor stopped Breslaw directly in front of the easel, then locked the wheels of the chair in place. A transformation came over Breslaw. His head rocking stopped and his focus went to the painting in front of him, Luka's life portrait still on the easel from the night before. He reached out and began lightly touching the finished areas of the work with his fingertips.

Luka walked around to the side where he could observe better. Breslaw's eyes were taking in every inch of the finished portions of the work, scanning and stopping over each detail as he brushed across it with his fingertips, as if recognizing the landmarks of an enormous map, checking them off as he went.

As Breslaw continued, the doctor pushed the palettes and paints up close to his side. until they just touched the little man. Breslaw moved his attention to the unfinished portions of the canvas. His hands and eyes scanned the white, open untouched areas, but they scanned deliberately, as if he were seeing details that were soon to come. Occasionally he would nod in recognition, then move to another unfinished area and began scrutinizing it.

Finally Breslaw moaned unintelligibly, turned to the worktable, and began squirting paints onto a hand palette. His actions were clean, deliberate and smooth, no longer those of a frail, worn man. He didn't seem to be wasting any motion, reaching for, and putting back each tube of color, as if he knew instinctively were they all belonged.

"You see," the doctor started, "when the colonel found out he was a painter, he was sent up to serve the officers. He lived a special separate life from the rest of the prisoners, part of a troupe of artists, singers, dancers, musicians; they would play and perform for the colonel and the other officers, during mess hall, for special functions, when Nazi dignitaries arrived. Things like that."

One hand holding the portable palette, with the other Breslaw pulled two detailed camel-hair brushes and one broad slant-cut brush from a jar of turpentine, dried them against a clean rag, and placed them in his shirt pocket, tips up. With one move he turned and pushed himself away from the table and rolled back to an empty spot of the canvas, just above the center. He reached in, grabbed the arch-cut brush, flipped it over in his fingertips, and began mixing white, crimson, and just a dab of black on a clean area of the palette. The mixture grew slowly into a small, thick pool the color of sun-bleached clay bricks.

"But Korzak was ornery, stubborn. WEREN'T YOU?" the doctor poked at Breslaw's shoulder. Breslaw wobbled in his chair at the intrusion but otherwise didn't seem to notice. "Most of the time he did as he was told, but every now and then he would surprise the colonel. One time he painted a portrait of a German shepherd collie leading a parade of SS guards, its paw up in a 'Heil' salute." The doctor was chuckling, slowly shaking his head. "It was quite good, really."

Now Breslaw was dipping into the new color, bringing it onto the brush hairs against the palette, then dabbing it in smooth strokes down the canvas. The color spread evenly against the pressure of his fingers. He would stop exactly as the color began to thin against his stroke, go back and pick up just enough, smooth it out against the palette, and pick the stroke of color back up from where he'd left off, then continue down the canvas seamlessly from top to bottom. There always seemed to be the right amount of paint on his brush. His work looked practiced and effortless.

"And the colonel doesn't put up with that from anyone, much less a Jewish prisoner," the doctor added with a snide tone. "He had Korzak locked in the hotbox, solitary confinement, standing in shackles all day. I can't remember all of his punishments." The doctor laughed out loud.

"One time, Korzak seemed to have fallen back in line, went for weeks painting what the colonel demanded. Then he was told to paint the archway over the officers' mess hall. It was supposed to be the Brandenburg Gate in Berlin, right across the top." The doctor gestured in a grand arc over his head. "But he painted the interior of a latrine instead!" The doctor laughed and slapped his knee. "In a single day; it was remarkable. The archway opening to the mess hall was the latrine hole."

Breslaw's strokes were exact; he didn't hesitate where he wanted the brush to go next, and he never stopped to back away and take in what he was doing. His moves were deliberate, sure, but rapid, with no hesitation. As he started each vertical pass beside his last one, he would go back to the palette and add just a touch more black to the color well and dab it in before starting his stroke. An oblong rectangle of brick-red was growing on the canvas, shaded so that it appeared to move from sunlight to shadow.

In his five years at art school, Luka had never seen an artist paint this fast, and because Breslaw never stopped to back up and survey his work, consider and reconsider, the piece grew at three times the speed a normal painter could realize.

"He was beaten badly for that one, across the back, but Korzak's good work was just a little too good, everyone wanted him. The colonel would have liked to have broken both of his hands, I'm sure, but now word had gotten out, and every ranking Nazi in the party was coming to see the paintings. His work was on display in the officers' quarters, and the colonel's apartment; some of the officers' wives even hung some of his best work in their own homes outside the camp. More than a few visiting dignitaries became interested in them, and gradually talk grew louder of shipping him away. I heard at one point, even Goering considered bringing him permanently to Berlin."

Breslaw dropped the large brush back into his pocket, replaced it with a fine one, and went back to the white, mixing it lightly with black and just a dash of plum on the palette. He then exactingly painted small fine horizontal and vertical lines across the deep red. As he went from left to right he would dab in just a bit more black and purple into the white.

"But the colonel had finally had enough. When talk of moving him away from camp started, Wirth sent him to me."

Luka stopped to look at the doctor as he talked. "Sent him to you, as a punishment? Why?" Luka asked.

The doctor stared back, confused. "It's the reason the camps have a medical officer." He answered, "Look...my staff has nurses to take care of the soldiers, and the day-to-day medical problems with the Germans, but we aren't taking care of the prisoners." He paused, looking for recognition, but Luka offered none.

Breslaw was now painting fine shaded straight lines across the red. Luka recognized the front facade of a brick building, flowing perfectly from sunlight into shadow. The perspective of the lines was exact, each slightly off parallel from the one previous to it, introducing depth to the scene taking shape. He had seen artists at school falter at the tedium of painting background like this. But Breslaw stayed intense, fast, and accurate; carefully watching his brush, then the palette, then the canvas. First long uninterrupted horizontal, then quick vertical lines recreating the mortar.

Luka looked back at the doctor, still waiting for an answer. "He was sent to me for experimentation," the doctor explained slowly and deliberately.

Breslaw chose a broad arc brush from the table. He turned to the palette, this time mixing ochre and yellow into a golden-brown. As he went back to the canvas he painted broad sharp strokes below and to the left of the brick facade.

"Experimentation?" Luka repeated back.

"Yes," the doctor confirmed. "It was going on in all the camps, hundreds of them." He paused, letting the words settle into the conversation.

"On...prisoners?"

"Yes, of course...on the prisoners."

Breslaw had replaced the big arc brush with a fine tip and was painting small pine-green streaks in radiating arcs. Luka recognized clumps of sage and Dallis grass on a sunburned bronze lawn.

Luka didn't speak, trying to take in both what was being said, and what was being painted in front of him at the same time. He glanced from Breslaw to the doctor again.

"Incredible research, really, into all sorts of areas. Different compound trials for diseases like tuberculosis and malaria. Research into dwarfism, comparative disease study in identical twins, exploratory open heart surgery, emergency battlefield procedures without the use of anesthetic." The doctor looked lost in his own explanation.

Breslaw had finished the lawn and was now painting a tattered fruitless pear tree in citrine, with fractured pieces of bark exposing the pale cream-colored raw trunk beneath. And suddenly Luka recognized the tree, and the scene, from behind his sophomore college dormitory.

"I myself was working in the area of stimulant neurotransmitters; most people know these are the adrenal stimulants—epinephrine and the like. Up until that time they had only been used successfully to revive people from heart trauma, by injection directly into the chest. But of course, the subjects didn't stay alive for long..."

Luka found himself slowly backing away from the easel, in sensory overload, eyes fixated on Breslaw and the magical recreation he was pulling from Luka's life. In his ears the doctor's words were ringing; he was hearing the doctor's soliloquy, but it seemed to be coming from far away, as if leaking in through a nightmare.

A deep explosion rocked the warehouse, raining dirt from the glass skylight overhead. The doctor jumped and winced in reflex. Breslaw didn't appear to be able to see or hear anything but the canvas and paints in front of him. He had finished the tree and was just beginning to paint a faded lapis splotch beneath the bottom of the tree, in the shadows. Luka knew instantly what it was, his mother's old blanket. He had rescued it from a box for charity donations after a Thanksgiving visit home his junior year and hauled it back to college with him.

He had spent that last week of August unpacking the new supplies that had arrived for the art lab. He and Anna were both helping Professors Mills and Pennington set up for the semester, to earn a little extra money, and perhaps get in good for the arts apprenticeship the coming year.

The building had been miserably hot, the air conditioning wasn't on yet for the semester, and he and Anna had unpacked boxes on what turned out to be the hottest day of the year. By the end of the day they all four of them were drenched in sweat, stinking from the day's efforts.

Afterwards he had wandered back to his hot dorm—didn't even bother with the shower— he had just wanted to be outside in whatever cool evening breeze he could manage to find. He grabbed an iced six-pack of beer and headed outside to cool off, carrying the old blue blanket to lie on.

He had headed right for the old pear tree, standing sentry in the nearly dead lawn, marking the dividing line between the boys' and girls' dorms. But as he went to sit down, he found Anna on the opposite side, her white shirt tied up in a makeshift halter to cool off.

They talked for hours on end, laughing until they were giddy on cheap beer, sweating under the tree as it stood watch over them in the hot evening with no breeze. He had loved the way the curves of Anna's hips peaked out from underneath her tight red shorts, the small yellow hairs on her arm that glowed like a golden aura in the moonlight.

They had made love there in the dead grass, with wild sweaty abandon beneath the tree, atop the old blanket. There out in the open, before anyone else had arrived on campus. It was brazen and stupid, sensual and wonderful; they had both simply let go into the moment, something that so rarely happened to Luka, before or since.

"...along with several other men were submerged in tubs of ice water." The doctor was still rambling on. Luka had lost track of time, wandering through the hallways of his past.

Luka stood staring at the section of painting as Breslaw added the final touches of detail, the wisps of Anna's blonde hair falling across his arms and the blue blanket. He had even painted small swatches of dead yellow grass dotting the blanket, exactly the way Luka would find it three months later when he went to unfold it on a cold November evening. Luka imagined he could walk up close and hear Anna's little girl giggle, maybe still smell the hint of lemon perfume she used to wear on her neck...

"STOP!" Luka yelled. The doctor looked at him, stunned at the interruption. "Enough of your bullshit. I want to know exactly how this is happening! How is it possible for him to see my past? How can he do...this?" Luka gestured to the painting. "What does this have to do with the concentration camp and your experiments?"

"You don't need to yell at me, boy," the doctor sneered. "You want to know everything, fine. Here it is." The doctor grinned, "but before I explain any more, come over here." The doctor gestured to Breslaw's chair.

Luka walked slowly back to the painter and the easel.

"Touch him," the doctor ordered.

Chapter 37

Luka slowly approached Breslaw's back. He glanced at the doctor.

"Go ahead, it's alright," the doctor answered with a wry smile.

Luka lifted his right hand and gently lowered it onto Breslaw's left shoulder. Breslaw arched his back and gasped a loud inhale, "Unnnhhhhh". He dropped the palette and brush to the floor with a loud clatter. Luka watched in horror as the man's eyes rolled back in his head. He looked as if he would never exhale, and Luka started to let go out of fear.

"NO! No, it's alright. Just hold him for a moment longer. Don't let him go just yet."

Breslaw slowly relaxed his arched back until he was seated straight again, and he turned his head to look at Luka. He had wild hazel eyes, and ever so slowly he exhaled as his eyes fixed on Luka's. The gaze seemed to suggest something was known between them, even though Luka didn't know what that something could be, and a smile began to creep across Breslaw's mouth.

Suddenly he swung around, back to the workstation. Grabbing for more brushes, and a new palette, filling it with colors.

"Oooh," the doctor chuckled, "now you've done it."

"Done what?" Luka asked.

"You'll see, soon enough. That was a good one. Now shut up, and watch. No more interruptions," the doctor commanded. "You want to know the truth, here it is."

Breslaw was painting a new scene far to the right, on an open area of canvas. Starting with a wide swath of gray, the color of granite dust on the top right, fading away to black to the bottom left, he painted even faster than before, but with the same control, the hint of a grin still across his face. Brush to palette, mixing color, brush to canvas, smooth clean strokes, his pace was quick, confident...inspired.

"Yes, Korzak was finally sent to me. The colonel was tired of his outlandish stunts; any other prisoner he would have shot or had gassed. I don't know, perhaps he just wanted a bit of revenge. But the colonel definitely didn't want to see him end up at some other camp painting for some other commandant, perhaps even becoming famous within the Relch."

Breslaw now had mixed orchid and gray, and he was painting wide vertical stripes across the back of the scene.

"At the time I was conducting experiments in hypothermia recovery, to help save our soldiers in the field. So many of our young men suffered frostbite on the push into Russia. I was determined to find a way to heal the body after it had succumbed to hypothermia. I would submerge the prisoners into pools of ice water for long periods of time. The prisoners, of course, would try to escape—a normal human reaction. But I finally devised a way to chain them down in the tanks."

The wide vertical streaks were now being highlighted with a mixture of white and gray, fading to black at the top.

Another explosion shook the foundation of the warehouse. The floor shuddered, paints and brushes rattled, and a skylight in the back of the warehouse shook from its frame and crashed to the ground in a loud shower of glass. Rain began pouring in through the now open hole in the ceiling.

"I tried all kinds of treatments, re-warming, injections of warm saline; sadly, nothing really worked, especially for the extremities. Even if a person survived, their limbs would quickly suffer gangrene from lack of circulation, and have to be amputated."

Luka was beginning to recognize the scene Korzak was painting, it was here, inside the warehouse. The dirty lighting of a rain-soaked day had been perfectly captured. Luka looked up from the painting, and he recognized the supporting columns against the far wall.

"I saw some interesting success with epinephrine, though, directly to the heart. Especially for cases of extreme low body temperature, a person could be brought back around from the lethargy and disorientation, even without external warming. Some awareness and comprehension could be restored. But always it was accompanied by severe pain as the body re-warmed; the nerve endings were so damaged from the frost, they would literally over-fire, and the subject almost always went completely mad from the intense pain."

Breslaw had finished the background and was now painting a rectangular shape in pale cream.

"But then I hit on the most novel idea. The target for re-warming shouldn't be the limbs—those were expendable; and it wasn't working in the heart, it should be the brain. So I decided that on the next subject, I would inject a combination of epinephrine and silver sulfate directly into the brain. Epinephrine to stimulate the brain and bring the person back to life from significant trauma, and silver sulfate to kill the nerve endings and prevent the severe debilitating pain, the over firing. That prisoner was Korzak."

The rectangular shape had become a small table. And on the table Breslaw was now adding swirls of red, the hue of wet clay.

"He spent almost twenty minutes in the ice tank submerged from the waist down. At first screaming hysterically, but quickly the shivering began. He soon slipped into unconsciousness, and ultimately into a coma. His body temperature was very low when we pulled him out, his heartbeat very faint; brain damage had certainly occurred. Then I injected the solution directly into his spine at the base of his neck."

Luka walked back to the side of the canvas while the doctor continued talking. He watched Breslaw and tried to imagine the horror of the experience the doctor was describing. But Breslaw was lost, immersed completely in his artistic medium, with no doubts, no distractions, just purpose and talent, and an intense vision that needed to come out.

"He didn't wake for days, so I monitored him with an encephalogram continually. Even though he wasn't conscious his brain activity was off the charts, far greater than what is seen in normal patients, and it was still that intense even though he was unconscious. I could find no documentation in any of the medical literature that matched what I was seeing."

Now on the canvas, in front of the painted table, Breslaw was adding small patterned checkers of goldenrod and dark cyan. They seemed oddly out of place, as if they were floating in space, but somehow they were strangely familiar.

"And then he finally woke. I had him observed for days, but all he would do was roll his head around, as if he was looking for something. He was a vegetable, a functional invalid like you see today, unable to feed or care for himself in any way. I recorded my data, and had signed the order to dispose of him when a guard found him one morning lying in a corner of the room drawing on the floor—he had found a discarded lump of coal and was drawing on the floor, pictures of the camp, the ice baths, the medical facility."

The checkers extended up and ended in a small curve, then out to the sides in two narrow strips; they ended below in a sharp interrupted line across the bottom.

"It was remarkable, we left him on the floor there with his piece of coal, and he drew for hours, completely absorbed. He would pee himself, go without food or water, he didn't appear to even notice. The next day I had colored chalks brought in, and the results were even more amazing. Somehow his innate artistic talent was still there, intact, but now intensely magnified; and even though he couldn't interact with anyone, he could still draw his surroundings. He knew what was going on around him."

Now below the checkers, Breslaw started painting a new line of khaki. And a chill raced up Luka's spine. It was him! Breslaw was painting Luka in front of the table, it was his khaki pants that he had on at this very moment. Luka looked down to his pants and back to the painting: the color was an exact match. And the checkered shirt, Luka recognized it now, hidden away in his backpack in the warehouse's apartment. That shirt hadn't even been out of the backpack yet! Luka staggered a step backwards.

"So I had notepads brought in and he was allowed to draw, whatever he wanted. Whenever his supplies were taken away, he would fall back to invalid, unable to interact with anyone, drooling and messing himself. But then we slowly came to realize, what he was drawing was what was most significant. In one case, for example, he drew the death of a prisoner in the ice baths, a particularly horrible accident. He had somehow seen all of the details of her death, even though he wasn't in the room. As if he had 'read' the whole experience out of the minds of the doctors and nurses that had witnessed it."

Breslaw had finished Luka's shirt and pants, but he had stopped painting the bottom of the right pants leg halfway up, stopping at the knee, and ending the pants frayed and torn, as if they had been ripped.

Luka's heart was pounding in his chest. He wasn't sure he wanted to see the end of what Breslaw had to show him.

"I found that he could paint the life history of someone without even knowing them, as long as they were interacting with him, or even in some cases just coming in proximity to him, he could draw their past, their life history, at least the momentous points in their lives. He could single out those people that had experienced significant trauma, and of course being a Russian Jew, in a prisoner of war camp, he began to be overwhelmed, out of control. He couldn't stop drawing. Even when we forced him to stop, he would go into wild rages, or severe depression."

Breslaw was adding Luka's bronzed legs and arms to the scene. One arm holding the side of the red clay, the other deep inside the center, just as he had learned to do in art lab in college.

"All of this was amazing to watch, to be sure, but then one day, a new guard that hadn't been in the medical facility for long grabbed Korzak to restrain him. He grabbed him particularly viciously, by the neck, and Korzak went into an odd convulsion that I had never seen before. I thought he had been physically injured, but later when he was allowed to draw, he not only drew the guard's past but also drew scenes that neither the guard nor anyone else had witnessed before. The final scene he drew was of the guard falling backward off of an elevated construction platform at the camp. And then, sure enough, three days later, the guard died in exactly that way, falling off of a construction platform that had no railing. He fell backward and struck a pile of rocks below with his head, died instantly. Korzak had predicted the future."

A chill went up Luka's spine. And not just at what the doctor was saying; Breslaw had stopped drawing Luka's right leg at the knee. What he had painted was a stub wrapped in a blood-stained bandage. Luka felt woozy.

"Well, after that, word spread quickly, not just within camp, but also outside of camp, what I had created."

"What YOU had created?" Luka repeated. He was now backing away from Breslaw and the work coming to life in front of him.

"Yes," the doctor reiterated matter-of-factly. "This is what I have created." He pointed to Breslaw. "And I can re-create it, with anyone."

At that moment the center of the warehouse was ripped open by an explosion directly above Luka's head. Glass, metal, and concrete rained down, burying him in a shower of debris.

Chapter 38

Sounds...Sounds floating in and out... pain, intense pain...right leg, head. Luka tried to concentrate, focus on the sound...but.

Fading...More sounds, hands grabbing, PULLING. OWWW!!! DON'T, NO! The pain was excruciating, but no words would come. The yanking and pulling continued. PAIN!...BURNING!...NO, STOP! And the pulling stopped, but the pain was still intense, burning. It ran down his arms, through his back, and into his right leg in great throbs!

"Can you hear me?" the voice was saying.

I recognize this voice.

Yes, I can hear you...wait, nothing's coming out, I can't hear that either. Can you hear me? Nothing. I CAN'T HEAR MYSELF!

"Can you hear me?" the voice repeated, it was close now. "Luka, it's Doctor Clauberg. You've been injured very badly. Can you hear me?" Whoever was talking was shaking him again.

OWWWWWW!!! I can't hear myself.

"You're losing a lot of blood, I'm going to apply a tourniquet." This is going to hurt.

BURNING   PAIN!!!...PLEASE   STOP...NO, PAIN!!! White, burning, blinding pain that won't stop!

"Please wake up! We need the shortwave frequency, we need to transmit the order for your smugglers to come pick us up. We've been hit. We need to go. NOW..."

Fading...fading...blackness.

"Is he dead..." a voice was asking.

Luka could hear the conversation from far away, coming through the void of blackness. He tried to will himself to open his eyes, to fight through the fog, where was he?

"I had to amputate his leg, I'm afraid he's not going to regain consciousness."

Who were they talking about? Luka tried to open his eyes again, but the blackness remained. He tried to move his arms and legs, but they felt enormously heavy.

"It's our only option."

"But what if he doesn't wake, what if he ends up an invalid too? We can't get out of here then."

"We've still got all the paintings." And then a long pause. "We just have to lay low, hope we're not discovered. It's our only option!"

And then Luka could feel hands on him, on his chest and arms. A sick feeling of panic suddenly overtook him, and he tried desperately to move. And then a sharp stinging pain at the base of his neck, and then consciousness slipped away again, like a heavy black blanket descending.

Chapter 39

Luka sat restlessly in the chair, chest strapped tight against the back of the wobbly stool, right leg dangling absently from the amputation. The silver sulfate made everything in his vision appear hazy and distorted, like looking through a permanent mist of gray; he couldn't focus on anything in front of him. But the epinephrine shot directly into his spine was worse. It made his heart pound and his breathing shallow so that he felt permanently ill; and his mind, it raced incessantly, he couldn't shut it off.

Whoa...going to fall. Flail arms, try and balance. Grabbing air, nothing to grab! Reach again, again, nothing there. Everything's a blur, try and look up, down. Shapes there, what are they, who are they? Whoa...moving, going to fall. Reach for that, right there in front of me, I've got it.

Luka flailed out and clutched the doctor's arm at random, held on tight. And in an instant, a dizzying whir of scenes began to flash before him, like a movie in his mind. Unlike his tainted vision, these were clear and sharp, in remarkable detail and color, as if he were standing witnessing the doctor through the memories of his life.

Momma, home, sister, school, studying, books and books and books, can't breathe and can't breathe and now in hospital—asthma, breathing treatments, very nice nurse, very pretty. I like the hospital, it's clean, I feel better, feel better here. School, study, and night, coffee and amphetamines, late nights and studying and studying. I can see it all, so clearly, like a photograph taken from every angle, like I'm there, in the picture. Uniforms, marching, the camps, barbed wire, dogs, guns, surgery, ice baths, and bodies and bodies, soldiers, power, and freedom, and the bodies, the bodies, THE BODIES. I created this, I created it again, see? I can do anything, and I can re-create it, with anyone. I can re-create it with anyone. I can re-create it with anyone.

The doctor had long since pried Luka's grasp from his arm, but the pictures wouldn't stop flashing through Luka's mind. His vision was still gray and blurred, but the images kept coming, replaying, over and over, with no way to stop them. They were so bright and clear. Luka was mesmerized.

Then the doctor pushed Luka's chair closer to the table, moved the tray of smooth wet clay close, and pulled Luka's hands onto it.

Luka jolted upright in recognition. COOL, WET, it's clay, red clay, I can see it, in front of me. Yes, one hand on the side for balance, the other deep inside. I remember this! INSIDE, INSIDE...yes, it's here, it wants to come out, the PICTURES. I see it, I can bring it out, I know what to do!

Happily, Luka went to work...

ABOUT THE AUTHOR

Lee Hansen is the 54 year old author of The Price of the Muse, his debut novel. He is a writer, poet, musician, and a high-tech marketing manager for a leading semiconductor device manufacturer. Lee lives with his wife and two children in Colorado, where he sits impatiently waiting to be discovered.

www.ingramcontent.com/pod-product-compliance
Lightning Source LLC
Chambersburg PA
CBHW062137170626
46813CB00002B/732